THE LIFE OF THOSE LEFT BEHIND

THE LIFE OF THOSE LEFT BEHIND

MATTEO B. BIANCHI

Translated from the Italian by
Michael F. Moore

Other Press | New York

Originally published in Italian as *La vita di chi resta* in 2023 by Mondadori Libri S.p.A., Milano

Copyright © 2023, Mondadori Libri S.p.A.

English translation copyright © 2025, Michael F. Moore

Published by special arrangement with Matteo B. Bianchi in conjunction with his duly appointed agent MalaTesta Literary Agency and the co-agent 2 Seas Literary Agency

This book was translated thanks to a grant awarded by the Italian Ministry of Foreign Affairs and International Cooperation.

Production editor: Yvonne E. Cárdenas
Text designer: Patrice Sheridan
This book was set in Sabon and Helvetica by Alpha Design & Composition of Pittsfield, NH

10 9 8 7 6 5 4 3 2 1

All rights reserved. No part of this publication may be reproduced or transmitted in any form or by any means, electronic or mechanical, including photocopying, recording, or by any information storage and retrieval system, without written permission from Other Press LLC, except in the case of brief quotations in reviews for inclusion in a magazine, newspaper, or broadcast. Printed in the United States of America on acid-free paper. For information write to Other Press LLC, 267 Fifth Avenue, 6th Floor, New York, NY 10016. Or visit our Web site: www.otherpress.com

Library of Congress Cataloging-in-Publication Data
Names: Bianchi, Matteo B., 1966- author. | Moore, Michael, 1954 August 24- translator.
Title: The life of those left behind / Matteo B. Bianchi ; translated from the Italian by Michael F. Moore.
Other titles: Vita di chi resta. English
Description: New York : Other Press, 2025.
Identifiers: LCCN 2024044618 (print) | LCCN 2024044619 (ebook) | ISBN 9781635424522 (paperback) | ISBN 9781635424539 (ebook)
Subjects: LCSH: Bianchi, Matteo B., 1966-—Fiction. | Grief—Fiction. | Suicide—Fiction. | LCGFT: Autobiographical fiction. | Novels.
Classification: LCC PQ4862.I177 V5813 2025 (print) | LCC PQ4862.I177 (ebook) | DDC 853/.914—dc23/eng/20240923
LC record available at https://lccn.loc.gov/2024044618
LC ebook record available at https://lccn.loc.gov/2024044619

To the survivors

"When the worst thing that can happen to you does, I try to be a friend."
—JOHN WATERS, *MR. KNOW-IT-ALL*

THE LIFE OF THOSE LEFT BEHIND

Someone called an ambulance. The doorman? A neighbor? I have no idea who had gone to the trouble.

I could tell because I heard the sirens blaring. I heard them growing nearer and then stopping, at full blast, right below my window, before turning off with a throbbing sound.

I know that it's useless, that there will be no extreme attempts to revive him, that it's already too late.

I am at the doorway.

From the windows, from the balconies, dozens of people are staring at me. Out on the landing, a huddle of neighbors. They say nothing, and look alarmed and confused.

I hear the voices of the paramedics climbing the stairs, their frantic footsteps. My apartment is on the fifth floor.

When the three men in white uniforms carrying a stretcher reach my landing, they're sweating and breathing heavily. The first one looks around for a moment. He notices the idle elevator at the top of the next flight of stairs. He rolls his eyes, turns to me, and exclaims, "Why didn't anyone tell us there's an elevator?"

The elevator.

S. is there, on the floor, and I was supposed to advise them to take the elevator.

I don't answer, of course. I can't.
The first of many times.
People will ask and I won't know what to say.
For months. For years.
Forever.

But did you know this could happen? Did you **notice** any signs?

Yes.

And you didn't do anything?

I mentioned it. To his family. To his friends.

What did they say?

They said not to worry, that he was only being dramatic, that he just wanted to scare me.

And you?

I was afraid he meant it; I could feel it.

We hadn't been living together for three months. We broke up at the end of August 1998.

S. still had my house keys. He had left behind most of his stuff (clothing, shoes, odds and ends) until he found a new place. Every now and then he would stop by to pick up something he needed.

That afternoon he called me at the office from my home. The call was short, civil. We didn't argue or fight—unlike our usual pattern in even the briefest of exchanges.

Before hanging up he said, "Anyway, don't worry. When you get back, I'll be gone."

I heard his words as purely informational. But they were a declaration, a metaphorical statement.

They were his farewell.

A mantra is passed from mouth to mouth. A spontaneous referendum. An unwitting conspiracy. A unanimous vote. A constant plea.

Move.

That's what everyone is saying.

My parents, my sister, my friends, my colleagues, the acquaintances who have heard what happened. Even strangers with whom I come into contact.

Move.

Get away from there.

In the first few days I'm fragile, very fragile. I don't even know if I'm still alive.

Yet there is an adamant determination inside of me. No, I'm not going.

No one understands. Why would I want to remain in a home that is flooded with memories? Infested with memories. The home where we lived together, where he took his life, where I found his dead body.

Seriously, how can you even think of still living there?

I realize quickly, immediately, that there's no point in explaining. No one knows what I'm feeling. No one understands these sensations, the black hole into which I've fallen. They offer me advice from a higher place, but I am somewhere else.

Like offering a glass of water to a man on fire and acting surprised when he refuses.

I wouldn't know what to do with your glass of water. Can't you see that I'm burning? That a palliative is useless, pathetic? Let me burn. Please.

The elementary prescription they propose is that I take a physical distance: to move away from my memories. They can't understand that I'm invaded by them. Drenched in them. Even if I moved to China, they'd still be with me. Not even an ocean or a continent between my memories and me would make a difference.

I am my memories. I am my life with him and his absurd death. This awareness is who I am.

Move.

I'm touched by their affection. They offer me advice in this competition whose rules they ignore. Like using an abacus to solve a problem of astrophysics.

When others do not or cannot understand, the only person you can listen to is yourself.

The more they urge me to leave that apartment, the firmer my resolve is to stay. How strange, at a time when I feel drained of willpower, of the ability to make a decision, when I defer every possible choice, when I can't even take responsibility for myself.

Eat something. Okay.
   Get some rest. I will.
   Move away. No.

I have no willpower left, except on this one point. Deep inside I feel that I have to stay. I can tell that the burden of grief (and anguish and loss and...) weighing on my shoulders would not be lightened one bit if I changed my address. It's not a home delivery you can avoid by moving, or a stalker you can shake by running faster. No: Rather than run away, I feel that I have to remain in place and confront it. What else can I do?

As if grief were a well in which to sink, a tunnel to be traveled in its entirety, until you reach the other side.

The fact that you can't see the light at the end, only darkness, doesn't hinder my awareness that this is the way.

I seek comfort in literature.

My lifeboat in the world.

I look in the bookshop, I browse the library (the Internet is still in its early days). There isn't much on the topic of suicide. Suicidal characters do appear in many novels. But a story dedicated to just that topic? There are, of course, psychological papers and sociological studies: where it happens the most, and why.

The only material I do find is about the victims, not us survivors.

And I am one of them. It is with them that I'd like to begin a conversation, get some help. Why doesn't anyone write about them?

Why do they ignore the grief of those left behind?

The day I go back to the office I try to behave nonchalantly toward my colleagues, even if I am a wreck: There are dark circles under my eyes, a distraught look on my face. I'm losing weight with shocking rapidity. Hard not to notice how dejected I am, for that matter. I don't even dream of concealing it. Everyone knows what happened, they can't avoid acknowledging and adapting to it.

They welcome me back affectionately, with sober but eloquent gestures. Some hug me. Some shake my hand. Some even pat me on the back.

I work at a communications agency. I write ad copy, brochures, catalogues, radio promos, editorial content.

I share my office with a colleague, Tiziana.

On the first morning I make an effort to resist. Then, at one point, I don't know why, and there probably is no reason why, I break down and cry.

Tizi looks up and sees what is happening. She isn't quite sure what to do.

"Oh, dear...," she says. Tears come to her eyes, too, but she holds them back.

She looks toward the corridor. Someone might walk by and see me.

She stands up, mercifully, and goes over to close the door. She keeps the spectacle private, chooses to take on the burden herself.

"Go home," she says, then she rephrases it as a question. "Why don't you go home? You came back too soon."

It's been one week since the death of S.

"Staying home only makes me feel worse," I explain, between sobs. "I need to get back to work, to keep my mind busy, otherwise I'll go nuts."

She approaches my chair, and from behind me she places a hand on my shoulder and gives it a slight squeeze. An ordinary gesture of closeness, of affection. Neither she nor I have ever been very demonstrative. We've been working together for years and get along quite well as colleagues. We like each other as friends, but neither of us is the kind of person who wears their heart on their sleeve.

We both realize that if she hugs me now, I'll never stop crying. But I have to. I dry my tears and swallow the lump in my throat.

"You can open the door back up."

"Are you sure?"

"I'm not, but open it anyway."

Our first smile of complicity since the tragedy.

I find myself compiling a spreadsheet on grief, and not as a figure of speech. Grief really is a system with columns of how much you can bear: I manage to tolerate a certain degree of suffering, but anything more would be too much. It would push me over the edge. Toward madness. I know it can happen. I've had proof of it.

Some thoughts are too excruciating to pass the threshold of consciousness. They remain buried beneath the surface, in a prolonged and protected limbo.

Every so often something comes to the surface: a conversation, an image, a fight, a scene of tenderness. All of which are equally merciless.

I'm in a tram on my way home after a long day at the office. Tired, drained, sitting on a hard, uncomfortable plastic seat, I look at the city bursting with life outside the window. And in that ordinary moment, for no reason, the memory of an argument comes back to me. S. saying, "Give me another chance," and me replying, "I've already given you a million chances, enough is enough."

The last fight the night before he left our home and went back to living with his mother.

I had repressed this exchange but now a sharp, vivid fragment of it returns. Give me another chance. No, enough.

He had asked me for an extension and I said no.

I'm a monster.

This awareness invades and shatters me.

S. was asking for help and I said no. I could have saved him and I didn't. I'm a monster.

I feel like I'm going to lose it. Here, in front of everyone, in a tram packed with people on their way home from work.

How much farther? A couple of stops. Four, five minutes. Resist. You have to resist.

I stand up. I make my way between the bodies and approach the exit. Let the monster out. I lean against the pole to hold on to something, not to keep my balance. I make it past the first stop. My own is getting closer. Now the tram feels very slow, moving at a snail's pace. I'm a monster. The last few feet are agonizing. The doors open, I jump out as if the tram were on fire. I walk quickly and break into a run. I want to be home, now, immediately.

I climb the stairs two at a time, insert the key in the lock, and give it a violent twist, hastily, time is running out, I'm almost there. I'm there. I'm inside.

I close the door behind me, slip off my backpack, and throw myself on the floor. I don't fall, I don't trip, I let myself drop toward the tiles, let the floor take me into its hard, cold embrace. Out rush the tears that

I've been holding back for all this time. Ten minutes of struggling to breathe. I'm a monster. Forgive me, S., I'm a monster. Forgive me, world. I'm a monster. I can never be forgiven for what I've done. I'm a monster, a monster. Help me, I'm a monster. Somebody please help me.

Before the funeral I receive flowers and cards.

One card is from the young couple next door. They're friends. Every now and then we would have dinner together. S. used to walk their dog; sometimes he would play with it on the balcony.

The card is simple, a single line, addressed not to me but directly to S. Which is probably right. As if I were only the go-between.

It says: "We will miss you so much."

Three signatures follow: Lori, Mario, and Camillo.

Camillo is the dog.

I don't know why, but this card touches me more than all the others.

I experience some physical changes, too.

They say that a person's hair can suddenly turn white after a strong emotional shock.
Something of the kind happens to me. The hair on my scalp turns gray. It was already going in that direction, but the process is accelerated. The emotional shock has aged me.

It's not just my hair. My process is more holistic than that.

A colleague runs into me at a business meeting a few weeks after the funeral, looks at me, and says, "You've really lost a lot of weight. What diet are you on?" She smiles, convinced she's paid me a compliment.
I try to smile back at her. "Well, it's a diet I wouldn't recommend to anyone." Only then does she recognize her gaffe.
"Oh my God, I'm so sorry…" She covers her face with one hand, she's truly devastated, but she has nothing

to be sorry about. Time passes, it's normal for others to forget the tragedy.

Those who can.

I'm the one who can't stop thinking about it for a second. A laser that is always on, night and day. Inevitable for my body to be affected by it.

I am becoming the grief that inhabits me.

S. and I met one night at a disco on the outskirts of Milan, even though neither of us likes to dance. That's not why we were there. I would occasionally step down to the dance floor where my friends were, swing my hips to the rhythm of a few songs, three or four max, and then get bored. S. didn't even pretend that he liked dancing. He would stand by the bar or lean against a column with a bottle of beer in one hand and have a look around. He was never alone for long. His shaved head, blue eyes, and forearms bulging from the rolled-up sleeves of his white T-shirt always attracted someone in the end. The confident, manly air about him was like rare merchandise in an environment where masculinity was vaunted through tattoos and roided muscles, snug wifebeaters, and skintight jeans. S. didn't need to show off.

Guys would find almost any excuse to hit on him. Have a light? Got the time? The usual banalities. Some even tried brazen come-ons, which he enjoyed puncturing. Like the guy who said, "I've been staring at you all night wondering what you're like in bed." S. answered, "Asleep." Or the one who's first line was, "I bet you're bi." S. nodded, and the other guy, "C'mon, let's go to my place, smack me around and beat me like you'd do to a woman!" And S., shaking his head, said, "Look, I always treat my women well." He wasn't one for long speeches. He preferred to cut to the chase. It was his way of asserting that he was who he was and not the fantasies that others projected on him.

Although I'd been to that disco several times and S. swore that he went there every week, we had never seen each other until that night. He was the one who approached me. He was thirty-five and liked younger guys. Everyone told me that I looked like an eighteen-year-old, even though I was twenty-five.

"Why don't we get together some night, away from here?" he asked me.

And I answered yes.

In my sentimental daydreams, I used to imagine falling in love with someone my own age. In my desires I imagined falling in love with a grown man.

Some desires come true.

The ten-year difference between S. and me made us worlds apart in terms of experience, maturity. When I met him, I was in my last year at university, had never had a job, and still had no idea what real life was. He, on the other hand, had a whole life behind him: a marriage that had ended, an ex-wife, a child to support, and a long résumé as a factory worker and manual laborer.

What I experienced with him has almost no connection to the silly games of my previous relationships, which had been little more than a series of parties, movies, train trips, and sappy kisses.

S. was resolute, practical.

He knew how to fix things. He had experience. He knew places to go and was comfortable around older people. He wasn't afraid of a challenge.

To spend time with S. was to spend time with a man.

He unsettled and excited me. He pushed me to grow. He accelerated me.

When we first started going out, S. introduced me to his favorite places. His personal map had nothing in common with mine, although we lived in the same province.

He took me on his motorcycle to eat at trattorias in villages outside the city whose names I had never heard and couldn't even pronounce correctly when I saw them on road signs. He helped me discover creeks where we could sun and swim without being disturbed.

He told me the stories of people he knew who, to my ears, sounded like characters from a novel.

Although we were contemporaries, we belonged to different eras.

His dimension was village life, the way things used to be: communities that were still solid where everyone knew everyone else and was serious about keeping customs and traditions alive. Mine was the bedroom community of a large metropolis, where modernity was within reach and our options (jobs, places to go at night, people to hang out with) were all projected outward. The only people there all the time were children and the elderly; the others commuted to the city on a frenetic, daily basis.

I understood dialect but I couldn't speak it. I only spoke Italian.

S. alternated between the two idioms instinctively, automatically. Walking with me down the streets of his village, whenever he ran into someone he knew, he would switch to dialect with an immediate, unconscious shift.

The ten-year difference between us seemed to get wider and wider. These cosmic distances fascinated me, making him even more irresistible.

("What the fuck are you doing with someone like me?" he would sometimes ask, still incredulous. I didn't know how to answer, but I did know that I couldn't live without him.)

Some love stories are born from affinity, from favorable circumstances, from common circles and friendships, from sheer physical attraction, aesthetic compatibility, shared ideals, a thunderbolt.

Ours was born on a dare, since nothing around us suggested it was remotely possible. Too different in our upbringing, social extraction, families, education, and culture.

But we decided that we didn't give a fuck. The very idea of not giving a fuck excited us. I keep asking myself today whether the challenge wasn't too great, seeing how things ended up.

But deep down we all know that the way a love story begins has no connection to how it ends. The two people who fall in love are different in the beginning from the two who break up in the end.

He hanged himself.

I still haven't said it.
It took me twenty pages to find the courage to write that down.

Word is going around the agency that the brother of one of the illustrators attempted suicide. He jumped out of a window but survived, God knows how.

I get word of it, too.

The life of an agency consists of a stable inner core and a galaxy of external collaborators, a muscle that expands and contracts, a revolving door of talent coming in and going out. Photographers, graphic artists, illustrators, directors, musicians, people who join a project and then disappear, and others who end up becoming permanent fixtures or repeat collaborators.

Roberto belongs to that cadre. A talented designer, with a poetic, almost childish brushstroke, bright colors, very pop tastes. He always meets his deadlines, a quality appreciated as much as artistic talent when a job is assigned to a freelancer.

He's here because they've asked him to do the illustrations for a new ad campaign, but he still hasn't gone in for instructions. He's come directly to me.

"Did you hear?" he asks.

I say that I have.

He tells me that for a few months his brother had shown signs of apathy, of depression, but alternating with days when he appeared totally normal.

"We knew he was going through a rough patch, but no one realized just how serious it was. I swear he didn't seem so bad."

He says this as if he has to justify himself. We share the same culpability; we misunderstood the same signals. I'm as much at fault as you, don't look to me to absolve you. That is what I want to tell him, but I let him talk.

He says that it happened at the seaside. His family has a small apartment in Liguria. His brother went there for the weekend, by himself, although he had said he was going with a friend. He jumped out of the window that same Friday, a couple of hours after he arrived.

He had planned on doing it there and couldn't wait any longer (that's what I think, not what he said). The branches of a tree broke his fall. He ended up with many broken bones and some nasty injuries, but he'll survive.

"I'm a wreck," he concludes.

Now it's my turn to speak.

"No, you're not. You're in shock. He's alive. I'm the one that's a mess, there's no way I can repair anything. You can still hug him."

Now it's me that Roberto hugs.

"You're right, damn it. You're right," he mutters while crying on my shoulder.

Only those who experience this can understand. Only those who experience this will know.

The first friendly face arrives right as the paramedics are carrying out the stretcher with S.'s body covered by a sheet.

It's Sara, my neighbor.

She's a psychiatrist.

She walks in, comes toward me, gives me a hug.

She says, "I was with him all yesterday afternoon. He gave no sign that he would do anything of the kind. I'm not telling you as a friend. I'm telling you as a professional."

Hers is the first attempt to reassure me that what happened was not predictable and above all that it was not my fault.

In the days, weeks, and months that follow, with ever-changing formulas, I will hear hundreds of similar attempts to absolve me.

A few minutes after Sara's arrival, two policemen come in. The paramedics must have called them. Or the doorman. I don't know.

They ask me a few questions. I answer.

One of the two notices the stack of envelopes on the table.

"And these?" he asks.

"They're the letters that he left."

The policeman picks them up, shuffles through them. "You do realize that we have to confiscate them?"

"No!" I say. I'm not saying it to them. I'm whispering it to Sara. I convey the information to her so that she can handle it. I'm incapable of arguing, of fighting, of begging. Sara understands immediately. "Please. They're for his wife, his son. It's the only thing that he left."

The policeman looks Sara in the eyes, and then looks at me. He is holding fragments of destiny in the form of sealed envelopes. He stands there for a few seconds without moving, then human compassion prevails over his professional ethics. Without answering he places them back on the table.

"Thank you," Sara says.

He nods and goes to the next room.

I had no idea of what happens in these cases. If I had to go to the morgue later on, if I had to sit for questioning, go to the police station...

Nothing will happen, at least not to me.

The family will be the ones summoned to the morgue. To identify him, to choose a coffin, to bring him home (to his mother's house, that is).

I had lived with him for seven years.

According to Italian law, I had no relationship to him.

I didn't exist.

Move.
>Leave.
>Go on vacation.
>Get a change of scene.
>See an analyst.
>Get a prescription for antidepressants.
>Confide in a priest.
>Become a Buddhist.
>Call a hotline.

The kind of advice I get.

Sara advises me to see someone who will help me. A therapist. A professional with whom I can talk.

She schedules an appointment for me with a luminary, her teacher, from whom she says she learned everything. The way she talks about him indicates an esteem bordering on adoration.

I trust myself. I place my trust in her.

I meet with him immediately.

It's been a few days since the funeral. I'm still in a state of shock, too deep in the abyss to envision some way out. It is premature to be seeking help now. I wouldn't know how to grasp a helping hand. I wouldn't even be able to see it.

And yet.

He gave me an appointment at the clinic where he works and is the chief of psychiatry. I ask for information at the reception desk, they indicate the floor, the room. I take the elevator, walk down the corridor, pass through wards. I'm a functional zombie.

When I get there, I find his name on his office door

but not him. A nurse sees me, asks me why I'm there, I explain, and she goes to call him.

From his agitation when he arrives, I get the impression that I'm tearing him away from some commitment, that he had to squeeze me into a very tight schedule, that he must have done it out of respect for my friend the psychiatrist, his student.

I'm a favor.

He invites me to sit down by his desk and asks what he can do for me.

Is there an answer to a question like that?

Yes: Nothing. No one can do anything.

"I don't know, doctor," I say.

"Sara told me what happened," he says.

For a luminary he's very young, fifty at most. I remember that Sara told me about a birthday party where he made a surprise appearance, that for her it was the best and most unexpected gift. A scientific authority still young enough to show up as a surprise at his students' parties. I imagine him with his sleeves rolled up, laughing and drinking a beer. My unconscious feeds me a random sequence of lives I haven't lived.

"I'm feeling so awful I don't know how I'll survive," I say.

He nods thoughtfully.

"It takes time," he says, "but you'll come out of it, of course you will."

He gives me a sort of clinical picture of what I'm experiencing at the emotional level, an illustration of my suffering, malaise, as well as methods to recover. He's exact, concise. He gives me examples.

A time frame.

As he's speaking a couple of teardrops descend my cheeks, involuntarily, like a sneeze.

He tells me that psychological support would help, but he's not the person to provide it, there's no room in his calendar at the moment.

I realize why a student might be drawn to a teacher like him. He conveys authority and solidity but without forgetting to appear friendly. But at the same time, to me the practicality of his advice sounds like a foreign language.

The session is already nearing its end. He shakes my hand in the same professional manner in which he performed his duty. Which he did, and probably did well.

I can't understand what this meeting was all about.

Five minutes later I'm outside. Alone. The city surrounds me with its incomprehensible, unstoppable vitality, screaming at me.

Muscle memory shows me the way home.

In the early days of going out, S. and I used to spend a lot of time in his car. Driving around at night we had discovered an abandoned building in the countryside a few miles from my town. All that was left of it were columns and a roof. Maybe the walls had collapsed or maybe construction on it had been suspended. Not that it made any difference to us. We liked the idea of this makeshift cathedral in the desert, the skeleton of a barn or warehouse that we turned into our secret refuge.

We would park underneath it, then stay in the car and talk for hours.

When it rained it was comforting to know we had a roof above the car. We could step out and still be dry while the downpour around us flooded the fields.

There are places that become part of our inner geography.

In later years, when S. and I had already been living together for quite some time, if we happened to drive by that area in the car, we would always cast a glance at that abandoned ruin in the countryside and smile at the memory of those nights.

It was inevitable that sooner or later, the structure would be demolished, and it was, a few months after his death. As if, with the disappearance of S., that ruin had lost all meaning to the rest of the world as well.

The truth is I'm glad that the skeleton in the fields is gone, the rickety temple that celebrated the dawning of our love.

Its demolition banishes any temptation for me to make a pilgrimage there.

I never reread a book. At least not from cover to cover. I might go back to certain pages, certain passages, when I want to refresh my memory of specific points, but only rarely do I do a complete rereading.

This was one such case. An American writer whom I'd read when I was young was making a comeback with new bestsellers after an absence of several years. I had rediscovered his first collection of short stories in a box at my mother's house and as I leafed through it, I realized that I didn't remember a thing. What the stories talked about, whether I liked them. Too much time had gone by. So I decided to break my personal rule by rereading the whole thing.

This was the book I had with me on the tram when I was returning home the night that S. died. The last words that entered my head were from its pages. Before the discovery of his body. Before the explosion. Before the void.

In my unconscious a link was created—senseless, arbitrary, relentless—between that book and my personal tragedy. Between the name of that author and my atrocious pain.

An accident of fate (because life is perverse, I realize) led to my meeting the author some years later. At a literary event in which we were both participating. We took a liking to each other and exchanged email addresses. Every now and then our paths would cross at some festival or other. Every now and then he sends me an email to say hello.

I never told him about his symbolic presence on the darkest day of my life. I don't know how he might react, what sense it would make to invite him into such an unpleasant coincidence. I'll spare him.

But whenever his name pops up in my inbox, a microscopic earthquake erupts inside of me, even today.

I have hardly any pictures of S.

Nowadays my cell phone would probably be filled with them, but we're talking about a time when cell phones had lousy cameras and the common meaning of "photo" was something dropped off at a shop to be developed and printed.

I do have a few albums (vacations, parties, snapshots of domestic life). Nothing to write home about, by comparison to the legions of images we're used to seeing (and producing) today.

The main thing is that I have no videos. Not a single sequence of S. that shows the way he moved, walked, smiled, spoke.

Not a trace of the sound of his voice. For young people today, this might sound unimaginable. It would probably fill other people, in my situation, with despair.

But not me, oddly enough.

If I close my eyes even now, I see him with complete lucidity: his smooth gait when he walked; the way he tilted his head when he spoke with me; his vivid and penetrating gaze; the wrinkles around his eyes; the lips that disappeared when he smiled. And I hear his voice, his laughter.

The absence of physical records doesn't bother me. His presence is hardwired into my brain.

I hate him. I hate him so much for what he did. How could he cast us into this nightmare? Me, his son, his elderly mother, his family. How could he?

You're a bastard, S., a fucking bastard. And a fucking egotist.

I shout it, alone, at home. I shout it at the walls of our apartment. Some evenings. Some nights.

I hate him. But at the same time I'm incapable of hating him. I mean, he's already punished himself so harshly: What would be the sense of adding my own wrath to that pile?

I'm torn between contradictory feelings, antagonistic forces that are crushing me: hate and love, anger and compassion, rage and tenderness, condemnation and understanding.

I can't even understand what I'm feeling. How can I go from one extreme to the other so quickly, at the same time, often within the same thought?

When you're adrift you don't float in only one direction. You're tossed here and there. And you're shattered in every direction.

At his funeral, one of the four pallbearers was his cousin. I don't know who told me, my memories of that day are fragmented and confused. My grief erased so much. I vaguely recall that S. had spoken to me about this cousin, who lived in the same town, their houses only a few hundred yards apart. The son of his mother's sister. Even if the cousin was about ten years younger, S. claimed that he was the only one in the family who looked like him.

I had never met him before. At the funeral I saw him for the first time and I immediately recognized him because, yes, it's true, they did look like each other. All of a sudden, the only thing I can focus on is this physical resemblance. I can't take my eyes off of him. I see traces of S. in his face, in his gaze, in the way he moves. As if a spark of S. were present in him, and that he's here, a few steps away from me, still alive.

I feel a mad, burning instinct to touch him, to grab him by the arm, to shake his hand, to pull him away from his job as a pallbearer, to get him away from that coffin.

I don't do anything. I don't move.

During the service I find myself looking in his direction every so often.

In his movements and in his expressions, I am searching for an echo of S.

While we celebrate his death, I seek a trace of his life.

I face this tragedy without a God.

I grew up in a Catholic family whose sense of the faith was always practical and concrete. My grandmother was a volunteer in the charitable works of the Church. My grandfather did the necessary repairs every time something in the parish was broken. My father's brother and sister both took the vows, dedicating themselves to missions in the poorest regions of central Africa for many years

For us, faith meant doing, not believing. It was translated into actions, not distant, abstract concepts. Not into ideal figurines to whom one was supposed to pray on Sundays and nothing more.

I had excellent models, but they weren't enough.

At one point I stopped believing. I can't explain when, in a vague interval between adolescence and adulthood. I realized that the conviction that people call faith was no longer present in me.

I took note of it.

The tragedy did not bring me back to God, grief did not turn me into a hypocrite.

I often asked myself whether this had made the moment more difficult for me.

I didn't have God to invoke, but I did not even have God to whom I could direct all my anger.

I don't know, either way, whether this was a plus or a minus.

When you're the victim of a tragedy like this, the only thing you want to do is put an end to it all. Take your distance from everything and everyone, and put an end to the agony with a single shot. And it's the only thing that you cannot do.

Because you have seen what it does to other people, the emotional damage that it leaves in its wake. You could never inflict on the people you love the living hell you're experiencing now.

A perfect contradiction, of a sublime cruelty.

According to statistics, every forty seconds there is a suicide somewhere in the world.

Every year more than a million people take their own lives (a number that surpasses the victims of homicide and of war).

The number of failed attempts is supposedly ten times higher.

In Italy alone an average of four thousand people die by suicide every year.

The World Health Organization has classified suicide as the twelfth leading cause of death in the world.

If we limit the field to the population between the ages of fifteen and forty-four, it becomes the third leading cause.

Statistically, women account for more suicide attempts, while a higher percentage of men succeed.

These numbers are generally considered inaccurate: The social stigma and taboo on an open discussion of the issue makes this information unreliable. Various suicides are probably classified (mistakenly or deliberately) as another type of death.

Yet despite all this data, this evidence from around the world, why is it that a person who survives the suicide of a loved one continues, desperately, to feel like the only one to whom this has happened?
To be specific, why do I continue to feel this way?

Whether or not they are aware of it, people **who commit** suicide drag you along with them. On that day, both of you took a leap into the void, and while there is no turning back for the first body, your own body has managed to get by unscathed. It's your spirit that's shattered.

In different ways, neither of you made it out alive.

You've never felt so alone.

You have never been so alone.

Among the many random acts of madness in the weeks following the death of S., there are also heartfelt confessions delivered to the wrong individuals, accidental victims.

I find myself telling people I barely know what happened to me, unable to restrain myself. After an ordinary "How are you doing?" they end up getting a shocking response, and struggle to react appropriately.

There were a couple of letters. A female friend whom I hadn't heard from in a while and an American professor with whom I'd been in contact about a publishing project. To each one I wrote a long, detailed account, one in Italian and one in English, telling them what I was going through.

Other people had sent me messages back then, and I don't know why I chose to open up to these two. With the friend it might have been a bland inspiration related to the confidences we used to share. With the American teacher there is no plausible rational justification. Blinded by grief, I was simply unable to distinguish between the reasonable and the inappropriate, between a confidante and a stranger. At the time it felt normal to open myself up to these two. It wasn't until a few months later that I found myself thinking back on it with absolute dismay. Needless to say, the professor did not write back and I never heard another word from him. The friend confided in me, when I saw her some months later, that the letter had upset her so much that she didn't know how to react.

Each in his or her way was an accidental victim of the situation. Every explosion strikes at random.

In the early days of our acquaintance, I tried to break up with S.

We had been seeing each other for a few weeks and neither of us had attempted to define our relationship, to give it a connotation, a name.

Our differences outnumbered the things we had in common. I enjoyed going out with him, but...

Was it curiosity? Was it a magnetic attraction between opposites?

Whatever it was, I was afraid that it would burn out quickly, so one night I tried to jump directly to an end that to me seemed inevitable, imminent.

I told him that maybe it didn't make sense for us to continue this way. In all sincerity I thought I was voicing his thoughts, placing on the table a question that we had been trying to avoid.

What I didn't expect, and what he gave me back instead, was a reversal of my convictions, a new start to the game.

He told me he was in love with me.

And that is how things changed between us.

One weekend in the mountains, close to the Swiss border, S. and I were guests of a friend. It was cold, snowing. Neither of us were skiers, but we enjoyed the winter-postcard atmosphere, the long walks in our boots, a few descents on a sled for a laugh, the evenings of mulled wine with the locals in front of a fire.

Our host placed us in a little lodge just outside of town. It had everything you needed: a heater, a small kitchen, and a loft bed, queen-size. But no bathroom. "For that you can use the woods," he told us, laughing.

The first night we were late going to bed, overcome by tiredness and alcohol. We fell asleep the moment our heads hit the pillow.

At one point, in the dead of the night, I heard S. get up.

"Where are you going?"

"I have to take a piss," he said.

It's December. Outside it's freezing. It's already gelid during the day, so you can imagine at night.

"You can't go outside like that. Put something on."

Summer or the middle of winter, it doesn't matter, S. sleeps buck naked.

"It'll take me a second," he offers by way of a justification, and goes out.

I lie there waiting for him to return. One minute goes by, then two. What the heck is he up to? I wonder. Why is he taking so long? I start to worry. It's so cold out there, I hope that nothing bad has happened to him. I'm about to get up when I hear the creaking of the door and the sound of his feet climbing the ladder to the loft.

S. gets in bed, a block of ice.

"What took you so long?"

He giggles, feeling guilty. "Since I was already outside, I smoked a cigarette."

"Are you crazy?"

He's amused by his escapade and slips under the covers with an unmistakable look on his face: He already has an idea of how to warm up. In a second, he's on top of me, pulling off my pajamas.

He's completely frozen while I, of course, am melting.

My memories of S. concern the seven years of life we shared. The moves from one apartment to another. Vacations. Road trips. Evenings on the sofa watching TV. Dinners on our microscopic table on the balcony... An avalanche of minutiae, each detail of which appears precious and, in equal measure, painfully irretrievable today.

My memories also include sex, of course. We were very much in love and filled with irresistible desire. In the early days we couldn't keep our hands off each other. Fragments of those moments have started to resurface, unconsciously, in dreams.

I woke up shaken and confused: The vivid image of the two of us embracing while we made love was consoling. It took me back to moments of great happiness and harmony, but at the same time it left me distraught to be remembering sex with a recently deceased person.

S. was dead and my body still desired him.

But was my desire really physical?

I didn't know and I realized that it didn't matter. I started to accept this, too: that remembering sex with him was another way of keeping his memory alive.

I discovered that, at such a moment, many barriers are ready to fall like dominoes if you pound your fist on the table.

I was in too much pain to raise moral quandaries.

As I thought of him, I started to masturbate.

I could still feel sexual desire for a body that had been a companion to mine for years and years and was now rotting in the grave.

I'm sick, I told myself. I'm not normal.

But I didn't give a fuck.

I kept on doing it.

For those few short moments we were still together, two bodies merging, penetrating, becoming a single being.

Sometimes I cried when I came.

I learn that I am a survivor. Not in the broad sense. Technically speaking. The relatives of suicides are called "survivors."

Like the survivors of a shipwreck, an earthquake, a war, a car accident, an explosion. Like someone who finds himself still alive, carrying on, when everything around has been swept away.

A survivor. Despite everything. Despite this.

Only thirty-eight countries in the world have active suicide prevention programs. In others the problem continues to be ignored.

For every fatal suicide attempt, there are an estimated six to ten survivors (parents, children, wives, husbands, friends), thousands of people who every year plunge into a state of extreme grief and mental distress.

According to the American Psychiatric Association, the loss of a family member through suicide is different from any other type of mourning. It is a catastrophic event.

There are currently no specific scientific protocols for assistance to survivors.

My great-grandfather Dorino, born in 1888, said that he had seen combat in all the major battles of the First World War. He was definitely a protagonist of at least two historical conquests: the battles of the Karst and of Monte San Michele.

A simple infantry soldier, he spoke, incredulously, of having witnessed the death, wounding, and mutilation of dozens of his comrades during the fighting. He himself remained completely unharmed. Not even a scratch, a surface wound from a bullet. Nothing.

He would always tell this story during Christmas parties, with the family gathered around and a few glasses of wine in his stomach. As he remembered the friends who had fallen, he would get emotional, unable to fathom his own miraculous destiny.

The most astonishing episode, however, came after the battles of the Karst and of Monte San Michele, when the entire battalion was sent to Albania. After the victories they won there, too, the troops received permission to return home for a few days. So at the port of Vlorë he boarded a ship headed for Italy, but a few seconds before the departure a group of officers arrived. To make room for them, some enlisted men had to disembark. Dorino was among them. His vehement protests against this unjust and unexpected change were ignored.

A few minutes after its departure, however, the ship was hit by a torpedo and sunk by the enemy fleet. Everyone on board died in the attack.

Once again, destiny had decided to spare him, and in the most obvious way possible.

Although I was very little, I remember my great-grandfather telling these stories and struggling to contain his emotions, even if I would not understand the substance of them until several years later.

I found myself reflecting on his stories and on his inexplicable fate.

Maybe it's inherent to my DNA: I'm destined to survive.

It's a legacy that runs in my family's blood.

Just like Dorino, who repeated his incredible story to anyone who would listen, I, too, have survived a war because it is my role to recount it.

"Now I have really known suffering. And I have survived...I have touched bottom. And I survive."

—SUSAN SONTAG,
AS CONSCIOUSNESS IS HARNESSED TO FLESH

My life is filled with music.

I've listened to music ever since I was a child, in a family that did not. It was at my insistence that a compact stereo system made its entrance to the house when I was still little, and it is also thanks to me that LPs arrived. (The first record I asked my mother to buy me was a single of Rino Gaetano, an emerging satirical singer-songwriter: not bad for the debut of a barely ten-year-old listener.)

I bought records with the first allowances that my parents gave me, saving enough money in a few weeks for an album. After I got my first job, I was able to go on buying sprees.

Over the years, my records have followed me with every move, from house to house. Today they occupy a bookshelf at the entrance to my apartment and a bookshelf behind the sofa. In the hallway one whole side is occupied by a CD cabinet. By now there are hundreds, I've never counted them, but I've never stopped adding to my collection.

I consume music at a constant pace, and always have.

I listen while I work, while I drive, while I cook, while I eat, and while I wash up in the morning.

I've had jobs in the music industry, written about music, worked in close contact with musicians. I don't know how to play any instrument. I have a horrible voice—I could never be a musician or a singer—but my life abounds with music. An authentic passion.

On only one occasion have I stopped listening to music: after the death of S.

For weeks I felt as if I were in a cosmic void in which my ears seemed to be ringing, like after a bomb goes off. A nuclear explosion in a domestic format.

Music irritated me physically, listening to it gave me no joy (or consolation, or calm). It had lost all meaning. Like everything else, for that matter.

I came back to it later. Slowly, like someone learning to walk again. Taking baby steps.

I start to believe that I am seeing S. Everywhere.

In a crowd, or a man racing up the subway stairs, a face at the window of a bus, a customer in a store who catches my eye through the shopwindow, a man crossing a piazza.

Sometimes there is a physical resemblance, in a quick glance at men, heads shaved, in their mid-forties. Sometimes it's a single detail: a green puffer, a baseball cap worn backward. Sometimes there's no correlation: I persuade myself that I've seen him, then I look more closely and see that it's no one in particular, a man who has nothing physically in common with his image. It's just me projecting traces of him wherever I look.

Sometimes I am convinced I have identified him in a person walking in front of me. That's the nape of his neck, I tell myself. Those are his shoulders. His jeans. The way he walks. Then I quicken my pace, get closer, pass him, and turn around for a glance. It's not him. No resemblance whatsoever. It can't be him, I know this before picking up my pace, before turning around to check.

Who am I trying to deceive?

Who am I trying to fool?

And yet these silly moments, the seconds in which I cling to the illusion that he's a few steps ahead of me, that he's still alive, that I'm about to meet him again, the second before I check—in that microscopic glimmer of hope, I start to feel better.

A flicker of serenity before plunging back into darkness.

What the survivor is seeking is not the remission of grief: He knows that's impossible. More than anything he yearns for a truce; he pleads for a brief armistice.

A few minutes with his head above the surface of the water, so he can start to breathe normally again, before sinking back into that eternal apnea.

I begin psychotherapy.

A psychologist was recommended to me. (In circumstances like these, support comes from the most disparate places: One person offers to spend the night so you won't have to sleep alone, another brings you presents, another cooks for you, and yet another suggests a good psychotherapist.)

I'm glad that it's a woman. At an unconscious level I consider her more understanding, more welcoming.

She's about ten years older than me, with short hair and glasses that she removes every now and then and sets on the table between us.

At our first meeting I tell her why I'm there. She says almost nothing. Me, I'm a torrent of words, trying to provide her with as many basics as possible, as if this were an oral exam where I already knew the questions and didn't need someone to ask them.

At the next session she confesses that when I left her office she started to cry, overcome by what had happened to me, by my suffering.

Her openness surprised me. She may have been violating her professional ethics, I don't think reactions like that are supposed to be shared with the patient, but I appreciated her showing how much she cared. Further proof, I thought, that she was the right person to understand me, to listen to me, to help me.

That's not how things worked out.
In the next few months, at weekly then twice weekly appointments, I remain stuck in a loop, constantly recalling the same situations, the same scenes.
I talk about the night of the suicide, my return home, my hand touching the body in the dark. I talk about the days that followed. I talk about the funeral. I always talk about the same things, like a drop boring a tiny hole. Especially the night of the suicide. I recall particulars that I might have neglected at previous sessions, details that accumulate in search of meaning. As if I had an insuppressible need to return to the same place, the same moment, and relive the scene in the most precise way possible, again and again. As if I never tired of it.

I don't cry. I talk, talk, talk, with no feeling.
I recall minutiae like a sadist chiseling at open wounds with a knife, and I never shed a tear.

I can sense her efforts to reach my emotions, so that I'll express rather than dissect them. I realize that something is jammed in the mechanism, never changing, a show that's still on the air but only in reruns.

The first few sessions I await my appointment with the therapist almost with trepidation. To know that there is such a moment during the week is comforting, sometimes it gives me a purpose. I leave the sessions feeling empty, yet somehow lighter.

Over time it becomes mechanical. A ritual. A commitment. That sense of lightness upon leaving becomes minimal, imperceptible.

One evening, at the end of our umpteenth session, without having planned it, I find myself saying, "There's no sense in my continuing, is there."

She has the honesty to admit, "No, I don't think there is."

A few days after I've gone back to live in the apartment by myself, my mother comes to pay me a visit.

In the elevator two women are chatting with each other.

"Did you hear about the tragedy?"

"The guy that killed himself? Yes, I did."

"And the other guy?"

My mother can't keep quiet. "The other guy is my son," she says.

She doesn't say it to defend me.

She doesn't say it to intervene in their conversation.

She doesn't say it to upset them.

She says it out of fear of what those two women might say in her presence. No matter what it might be.

The two women turn to stone, in fact.

The doors open.

My mother steps out.

I'm the other guy. The one left behind.

What will people say about me?

Like my mother, I don't want to know.

Elevators foster unforeseen intimacies.

One morning when I arrive at the agency, I find myself in the elevator with an art director who has been there for a few weeks, a man I barely know. During the ride up, we are both silent, our eyes focused on the closed doors. Without looking at me, he decides to break the silence. "Since we've only just met, I suppose you don't know that I'm very religious. Lately I've often prayed for you."

He is sharing a confidence as if it was a piece of information.

"Thank you," I say.

"I can't imagine how it feels to bear what you're dealing with," he concludes. Then, with a sad smile, he gets off the elevator.

The tragedy has made me famous. My colleagues devote thoughts and prayers to me. They see my abyss and realize how privileged they are to have been spared, how lucky that it did not happen to them.

I get a phone call.

It's a writer I know. I wouldn't call him a friend since we don't hang out together, but he is an author whom I've always admired and whom I'm honored to have as an acquaintance. Which he knows. I first confided it to him at the presentation of one of his novels, where I had arrived with a backpack full of his old books so he would sign them for me.

Maybe three or four weeks have gone by since the death of S. He has just learned of it (I don't know from where).

He asks me how I'm doing. He shows me affection and that he cares. We make small talk, leaving more profound matters between the lines.

Then, all of a sudden, in a complete change of direction, he asks, "Are you taking notes?"

If someone else had heard this conversation, they would have been floored by that question, seeming so completely disconnected from everything we'd been saying. Which notes? About what?

But I know exactly what he means to say. The level of our conversation has shifted.

"No," I admit.

"Do it."

"But—"

"Sooner or later you're going to write about this moment. Even if it might seem absurd to think about it now, deep inside you know that you will. We're writers. Writing is our way of articulating our experiences, of coping with life."

Of all the phone calls I'd received in those days, this is the one I remember most clearly. Because it came from a person who was distant but present. Because he didn't try to console me, knowing that I was inconsolable. Because he didn't use hypocritical formulas or beat around the bush. Because in the total darkness into which I'd fallen, he reminded me of the direction I would have to take one day to find my way out.

Two weeks before he took his life, I went to see his sister. She was the only member of the family with whom S. had a normal relationship. The two brothers he never saw or heard from. He never mentioned them, as if they didn't exist. Back when he was still married, their respective families would occasionally spend time together, on holy days of obligation. His separation and decision to live on his own (first) and with me (later) had alienated him from their vision, erased him from their radar screens. S. had reacted by erasing them from his.

With his sister things were different. There was a meaningful bond between them. On a couple of occasions she had even invited us to dinner. She was a single mother, separated, with two teenage children to raise and restrain.

It was strange to see S. in the role of uncle. Every time we went, the kids would look at him initially with a vague wariness, but over the course of the evening they would shed their reticence and rediscover the camaraderie they had always had. I understood them, anyway, it's not easy at a delicate moment in your hormonal growth to see your uncle pass from the role of paterfamilias to a gay man living with his lover. A guy like him, the very picture of male virility. It must have confused them quite a bit, at least in the early days, but then they got over it, because S. was clearly their favorite uncle, the funny one, the clown, who challenged them to silly contests on the playground, who let them drink beer when their mother wasn't looking, who told them dirty jokes and took them for rides on his motorcycle. It was obvious from their conversation that there was no comparison to the other two uncles, whom they basically considered to be idiots (an opinion I shared, although I'd never met them).

It was the first time I'd gone to Elena's without S.

To tell the truth, I had no idea where he was that night. At first, after we'd broken up, he'd gone back to living with his mother, but then I learned that even that arrangement wasn't regular. He often slept away from home, at friends' places, or maybe even with randos he'd hooked up with at the clubs. A couple of times, I came to find out, he'd slept in his car. All red flags of how troubled he was.

I went to Elena because I was so worried about the situation. When S. spoke with me on the phone, he would go from being conciliatory to shouting and insulting. Telephone calls between two people who are breaking up, that knot of hatred, resentment, affection, desire for reconciliation and longing for the relationship to end, the need to blame everything on the other person, the gratuitous desire to hurt them. All the ingredients were part of the norm. Except for one: the threat to commit suicide.

The first time he said it I laughed into the phone. "Cut it out, give me a break." I had taken it for a taunt, one of the many. Then he said it again, on a later phone call. I continued to play the tough guy, "I'm not falling for that," but something ominous was starting to emerge.

Which is why I was at Elena's for dinner alone, without S., and without even her kids, who were at an evening soccer match, to watch or to play, I didn't ask.

"He's just being dramatic."

His sister sipped her coffee, acting completely serene about the issue.

I had waited until the end of the meal to bring up the question and disclose my fears. She laughed at it, as I had the first time.

"He's never mentioned anything like that to me, give me a break. He knows I would never fall for it."

"Falling for it is beside the point. I tell him the same thing, to stop with all the bullshit, that no one believes him, but when he starts up again, I wonder: What if it's a cry for help?"

"Do you want my opinion? I think he only wants the two of you to get back together."

"No, he doesn't. Believe me. We've been going back and forth for two years now, this time there's no going back. It's over, and we both know it."

"Whatever, have it your way…"

"But that's exactly why I'm not the right person to be close to him at a moment like this. We can't even talk on the phone without insulting each other, we're obviously incapable of helping each other. With time I imagine we can go back to speaking civilly, maybe even hang out as friends, I don't know, I hope so, but right now we're at each other's throats at the drop of a hat. But you, instead—"

"Me, what?"

"You could try to be there for him, try to understand where he's disappearing to at night, keep an eye on him, make sure he doesn't do something stupid…"

Elena assumed an irritated expression. She stood up and started to clear the table, putting our coffee cups in the sink. She seemed to be buying time to formulate an answer.

"Listen, I've got troubles of my own to take care of, I haven't got the time to deal with your bullshit. My brother took all the liberties he wanted in life and is perfectly capable of managing by himself. He's not a child. Quite the opposite. He's capable of destroying a family so he can chase his desires, not giving a fuck about anything or anyone. So he's hurting right now? Poor baby. Do you know how many people he's hurt?"

Our conversation had taken a wrong turn. It had become almost accusatory. S. hadn't left his wife to be with me. They had divorced at least three years before we met, but now that detail seemed irrelevant. Even if he'd had a series of flings before me, I was the first and only man with whom he had decided to live. I was guilty of having made unequivocal a condition that, until then, his family could pretend to ignore or try to hide.

Elena was the only person in the family with whom I had a real relationship; we were in regular contact, treated each other affectionately, and it was strange for me to hear her saying things like that. She must have been tense and maybe already exasperated by this story. Now I didn't know how to respond to this shift in tone on her part, to this sudden rejection (you made your bed, now lie in it).

"Then what if something awful happens?" was all I managed to ask.

"What do you think will happen? He only wanted to scare you, and from the looks of it, he succeeded."

She laughed again, but it was a forced laugh, overshadowed by her outburst of prejudice

Maybe she's right, is what I thought then. Maybe S. is only being selfish, and his sister is as fed up with his bullshit as I am. It's normal for her to end up feeling that way.

A moment later that burst of anger was gone.

At the door we hugged each other and said good night with our usual affection.

I'm just being stupid, I told myself as I got back in the car. S. is playing around with me, like he always does, and I'm falling for it, I told myself. Stop letting him get the better of you, I told myself.

The last year that S. and I were together was like Chinese water torture.

Anyone who has experienced the end of an intense love story knows how painful and confusing and protracted and destructive and agonizing it can be. I don't have to explain anything.

In those months S. and I continued to live together and to hurt each other, unable to make up our minds to leave each other once and for all.

Arguments, violent arguments, were constantly breaking out over nothing. It was like balancing on a tightrope over an abyss—one wrong move and you fall. The shouts, the recriminations. We couldn't stand each other anymore.

I remember one night, after yet another quarrel, that S. went out and didn't return. I went to bed without waiting up for him. He came back in the dead of night and we started fighting again, immediately. I asked him where he'd been at that hour, and with whom. He claimed that he'd simply gone for a ride in his car, to clear his head. And then, in a fury, he started to take his clothes off, I was sitting on the bed and he was standing as he removed his T-shirt, shoes, socks, jeans, and boxer shorts, and then he stood in front of me, stark-naked, and ordered me to touch him, to smell him. To prove to me that he hadn't done anything, that on his body there was no scent of sex, no scent of another man.

Maria Teresa, a colleague, invites me out to lunch. She also knew S. She had called him about painting her house, they had occasionally hung out together.

She takes me to a trattoria behind the office. We sit at a table in an area set off to the side. The actual dining room is located in the rear, here at the entrance there are four tables that people choose only when all the tables in the main room are occupied.

We start to eat and I tell her what happened. By now it's a script that I can recite by heart. It's almost automatic. Then I'm overcome by emotion. I stop eating, I stop telling the story. I start to cry. Maria Teresa squeezes my hand. Her eyes are also tearing up.

At the table next to us there is a man eating by himself. A professional in jacket and tie, maybe a teller from one of the many banks that proliferate in this neighborhood, or some kind of manager. Fortyish. Receding hairline. He notices that I'm crying. He looks up from his plate and sees me. Not a quick glance: He's staring at me. At first his gaze is almost amused. A man crying in public: He must think that it's embarrassing, ridiculous. I couldn't care less, of course. I'm beyond good and evil, beyond the reach of people's opinions, beyond concern about what's appropriate, about the criteria by which some behavior is considered socially acceptable and some is not. I am my suffering, nothing more. Crying is my signature, my identity. The rules of the world no longer apply to me. You want to look? Then look.

The grin disappears from his face. He doesn't find me amusing anymore. Now he's curious. He wants to understand why I'm crying. He won't look away, my tears are his entertainment: At night he has dinner watching TV, today he's having lunch watching my agony.

He doesn't show the least restraint, I'm offering him a pathetic spectacle and he intends to fully enjoy it.

Maria Teresa has also stopped eating. This isn't the kind of conversation that whets the appetite. She proposes that we leave. I agree, to make her happy, not because I have a preference. When you have to cry, one place is as good as another.

As I stand up, I turn my gaze on my viewer. Not even direct confrontation intimidates him. He continues to stare at me unabashedly.

Once I'm out on the street, I look back one last time through the window. He's still there, following me with his eyes: He can't fathom that I have the audacity to cry on the street as well.

He hanged himself from a pipe that was located above the front door.

When I came home that night, I reached out my hand in the dark to look for the light switch and found his body dangling.

Before any of the other senses, I perceived the tragedy by touch.

It took a few seconds for my mind to grasp what had happened.

And a few more for my voice. I tried to shout but I couldn't breathe, no sound came out.

I struggled, in vain, before finally releasing the true howl.

They preferred to shield his mother from the truth. She's more than eighty years old, the news of her son's suicide could have had emotionally devastating consequences. The official version they gave her was that it had been a heart attack.

"Such a strong man, so healthy," she kept repeating on the day of the funeral, disconsolate, having a hard time believing what had happened.

Everyone nodded, going along with her and playing their part. These words, which others saw as the naïve commentary of an ignorant mother, did not sound at all inappropriate to my ears. In a sense they were another form of the truth, because S. really was strong and healthy, which made his act even more horrifying. A rejection of life by a man whose body was bursting with it.

S. brimmed with vitality.

He could never stay put. He was always running around, speaking with anybody. He knew everybody.

One summer we went on vacation to a little town on the coast of Spain. On the third day, in the late afternoon, as we were walking back from the beach, he said hello to everyone we ran into on the road. The tobacconist, the baker, the news vendor. S. didn't speak Spanish, or English, or any other foreign language.

"How did you meet all these people in the two days we've been here without knowing the language?"

S. shrugged his shoulders. "I still managed to communicate," he said.

One morning we entered a crowded subway car. In all of five seconds, I turned around and there he was, talking to a stranger.

"Will you please tell me how it is you're able to start a conversation so quickly?" I asked him later.

"It wasn't me it was him," he explained. "From the tattoo on my arm he could see that we'd been in the same military corps so he said hi."

Even when he was silent, S. drew the attention and the remarks of strangers.

A magnet for the conversations of the world.

In grief there is a before and an after.

Before, I used to be another person.

I will always wonder whether the real me was the carefree youth of before or the broken adult that came after.

After many years at the advertising agency, I left to pursue a career that was in constant flux. I collaborated with a wide variety of businesses: newspapers, radio stations, publishing houses, audiovisual production companies, television stations, creative writing schools.

Time passed and I found myself being introduced to new and always different professional realities and colleagues.

The precariousness of creative work means that you are in a constant struggle to start from scratch every step of the way, but it also allows you to continually reinvent yourself. A serpent that sheds its skin time after time. I was a different person and the people around me had no way of knowing who I had been previously. I told no one about my past, about what had happened, about S. I lived exclusively in relationship to the present, to the new facade.

With time grief became more and more intimate, more and more personal, a secret hidden in the recesses of my soul. Like the echo of a torture, like a mysterious treasure. With time it became more mine, and mine alone.

"Grief turns out to be a place none of us know until we reach it."
—JOAN DIDION, *THE YEAR OF MAGICAL THINKING*

I am constantly using the term "grief," although I know it's inappropriate, since it refers only in part to what a person is feeling.

Alongside grief there is an ongoing sense of disconnect from the real, as if between the world and me there were a sheet of glass, a subtle but concrete distance that turned me into an outside spectator. As if I were perennially somewhere else, in a place I had never been, a private and unreachable abyss.

I felt something like the opposite of omnipotence: You do not know where I am. You think you can see me, but I am deceiving you. Please, carry on with your business. The ordinary things of this world no longer concern me. Now I have known true darkness.

There is a kind of arrogance in pure grief.

Grief is an anesthetic. It wraps around and protects me. It even makes me invulnerable to the cruelty of the world. People can say anything, do anything to me, I don't react, I don't care.

I find out that I'm not afraid to take risks anymore, I can cross dangerous areas at night by myself, ignore guns pointed at my face or knives at my throat, be as invincible as a superhero.

On the television I hear the news of a man who during a bank robbery confronted the criminals alone, offering himself as a hostage in the place of the little girl they were holding.

They say he's a hero.
I think to myself: Is that all it takes?
Send me instead.
The worst has already happened.
Nothing else can hurt me.

I discover that I've become immune to fear.

At night, in bed, unable to sleep, I wonder what I'd be willing to do to see S. again, to have the opportunity to speak to him one last time.

I don't know why, but a crazy idea occurs to me: to be given the opportunity to meet him *as a dead man*. That the door will open and he will walk in like a zombie, giving off the first whiff of putrefaction, with strips of skin hanging off his arms, making jerky, unsteady movements, with terrifying guttural sounds coming from his open mouth in an unnatural, hideous manner.

And inside myself I think: This, too, would be acceptable.

I could bear it.

Please, all I want is for you to let me see him one last time.

But not even the demons of the underworld heed my laments.

A French television series from 2012, *Les Revenants*, created by Fabrice Gobert and based on the film of the same name directed by Robin Campillo, is a hybrid, with elements of science fiction, thriller, and horror. The screenplay of the first two episodes was written by one of the masters of the French novel, Emmanuel Carrère.

I still remember how I felt when I saw the first episode. I didn't know exactly what the plot was, having read only a couple of rave reviews that aroused my curiosity, so I downloaded the whole series illegally from the Internet (it didn't arrive in Italy until one year later, on the strength of its international success).

At first the atmosphere was typical of a thriller (creepy music, underpasses at night, gloomy and threatening), so I expected that type of story. But when I came to realize what the subject was, I started to feel my heart beating faster, my breath becoming strangled, and tears streaking down my face.

The story is set in a small town in the Alps, where out of the blue dead people start to return home. Unlike classic horror films, in which a character who returns from the realm of the dead reappears as a zombie, here the characters look completely normal. They appear exactly the way their loved ones remembered them, as if they had been frozen in time. They have the same haircut and same clothing, and are the same age as they were on the day of their passing. The most disturbing figure was a teenage girl who had died in a road accident, and when she returns, she finds that in the meantime her twin sister has grown and is now nearly twenty years old.

The presence of the revived ("*les revenants*" of the title) causes a shock to all the families involved, with discordant feelings and reactions, and creates predictable havoc throughout the town.

Les Revenants spoke to a very deep part of me, going beyond the trauma and the characters in the series, beyond the space and time in which it was set. I am sure that for the average viewer it was simply a good mystery with Gothic overtones. For me, a survivor, it was the representation of my most intense and unrealizable desire: the return of S. And not a monstrous S., transformed into one of the living dead, not a ghostly S., a holograph verging on hallucination; no, the normal S., the S. of the last day, the S. for whom I had so many questions, so many explanations, forgiveness to beseech, hugs to give.

I watched the whole first season in an almost feverish state. At the end of each episode my face would be lined with tears, regardless of whether its contents were frightening or conciliatory: I cried all the same. For me it was not an evening entertainment but rather a spiritual experience, a mystical science fiction in which the message was lost to the normal public (and probably went beyond the intentions of the authors themselves), but that found its perfect recipient in me.

I have seen many other television series over the years, but nothing ever hit that close to home. Perhaps in part because the experience was so personal: Where other viewers might have seen horror, I was witnessing a private communion of the body and the spirit, of conscious and unconscious language, which found perfect harmony in a symphony that only I could hear.

I suppose it's only natural to indulge yourself with the thought that it would be impossible for a loved one to die by suicide, to feel that it might happen to the (devastated) lives of others but not to your own. Dwelling on the thought more seriously might simply be too terrifying.

This is why in practice we tend to ignore it, even if this theme is as present in art as it is in the daily news.

In the weeks after the death of S., I ask a friend, a big reader, to suggest some escapist literature, something to take my mind off of things. He gives me a novel by a British author, a romantic comedy set in the world of music, which I start to read almost as an exercise, and which does in fact manage to keep me occupied. What a shame that here, too, toward the end of the book, one of the characters commits suicide.

When I point this out to my friend, he is crestfallen. "I completely forgot that detail!"

Poor guy, he's not to blame. Obviously for him it's a simple plot twist, a detail, as he put it, something that would not linger with a normal reader.

Until a short time ago, I was like him, and I would never have imagined that one day I might think differently.

The extreme act of taking one's life is present in **books**, films, television series, plays, and even in some **songs** of summer, and for all of us it's normal to **not even** notice it.

I realize that I'm synchronized to other frequencies, struck by details that used to leave me indifferent, and see things now that used to be invisible to me.

Even ordinary things on the radio end up moving me deeply. The refrains of pop songs take on new meaning, they stop being merely entertaining and start to become substantial.

At a clothing store, as I'm wandering through the items on display, I overhear "No Regrets," a song by Robbie Williams. I am struck by the words and their meaning:

I don't want to hate,
But that's all you've left me with...

No regrets now, they only hurt...

At a festival in the piazza, from the loudspeakers I hear Gloria Gaynor singing, "*I should've changed that stupid lock, I should've made you leave your key.*" I was constantly thinking the same thing. The very same words.

I'm driving, Cher is singing to a dance beat and I find myself asking philosophical questions.

"Do you believe in life after love?"

To my ears this sounds like: Do you believe you can survive all this?

I don't know, girlfriend, I really hope I can, but I don't know how to answer.

Anesthetized receptors are active and alert once again, a search for meaning that travels in every direction.

A few days after the funeral, I come to find out that one of his brothers is going around saying that he wants to wait for me downstairs and beat me up.

One of the two brothers who during the years that I lived with S. never spoke to him once, not a single phone call or text, and even refused to acknowledge that we were a couple, saying that he was ashamed of S. Now, after his death, he has rediscovered their bond and is blaming me for everything. I supposedly ruined him, destroyed him, and since no one has the guts to speak with me, he wants to resolve the matter by teaching me a lesson to the rhythm of his fists.

Let him, I think. Go ahead. Nothing can hurt me anymore.

Come forth from the darkness, my enemies. I'm not afraid of you. Attack me. Strike me.

You cannot imagine how invincible I am in this moment, how nothing frightens me.

At night, in front of the main door to the building, I look around to see if a silhouette is crouching in the shadows awaiting my arrival.

No one ever shows up. Cowards.

With Angela, his ex-wife, I have an ambivalent relationship.

When S. and I started dating, he had already been separated from her for years. I wasn't the cause of the scandal, the home-wrecker. The family had done all the wrecking by itself.

(From a conversation I had with S.:

"Did you leave your wife because you realized you were gay?"

"No, I left her because I realized that I didn't love her anymore. Sex with men had nothing to do with it. That came later.")

Over time there were a few opportunities to meet, usually when S. went to pick up or bring back their child. Nothing too theatrical, no dinners with the extended family, we didn't pretend to be more modern than we actually were. I respected her limits and in exchange she expressed some friendliness toward me. No apparent friction.

But later.

On the day of the funeral she goes back to playing the role of the wife, the widow. For society she is the one in mourning. They ignore my existence. I'm just a friend, in the twelfth row.

Grieving, but in the middle of the church.

Far from the coffin, far from the relatives.

Almost everyone in the family is aware of my existence. No one, on that day, is willing to concede to me a role, a place.

At the end of the ceremony, for a second, Angela and I cross paths.

I extend my hand, a single gesture of sharing her grief.

She looks at me, coldly, and does not extend her hand.

My hand remains there, inert, pressing on an inconsolable void.

I should hate her for this, but I don't care, I really don't.

We're both distraught, who cares about formalities, about malevolent looks. I've learned that grief justifies everything. Even an act of momentary pettiness.

Time finds a way to heal all wounds.

A few weeks later she calls. One night, in tears.

She says, "I'm calling you because you're the only one who can understand me. The others are family, it's different. We two are the only ones who know what it means to lose him because you and I were in love with him. We loved him as a man."

The maturity of her words erases years of prejudice.
This is the hand she is finally extending.

As a child, as a boy, I could only fall asleep if the room was pitch-black. If even a tiny glimmer of light filtered through the slats of the blinds, I would get up and go over to close them completely. The night had to be absolute for me to sleep.

Then I started to travel, to sleep out, to find myself in circumstances in which I could not control the degree of darkness in the room. I had to adapt. The first few times it was difficult. (I still remember one awful night in a room without blinds, in northern Germany, I think: the streetlights, the daylight invading the room at dawn...) With time I became more used to it.

Now it's no longer a problem, I've learned to sleep regardless of the lighting situation and when I think back on that youthful obsession, I find it idiotic.

Proof that you can get used to anything, even to what once might have appeared impossible.

In the months following the tragedy, I keep repeating ad nauseum, in an attempt to force myself to believe it, that I'll learn to live with grief, that I'll get used to the emptiness inside that like a black hole sucks the life out of everything. A day will come when this gash will be just another facial feature, a part of me that is no longer upsetting.

    Like the way I walk.
    Like the fact that I don't eat fish.
    Like that I'm five foot five.

The things that make me me.

It's not easy to talk about. For others.

I can see that it's difficult for them, that they're looking for the right words, the proper tone.

How should some things be addressed? No one prepares you for it.

It's a delicate gesture that we have to improvise.

But some people have no qualms. Only later, in retrospect, does this become clear to me. At that moment I endure it without reacting. I answer. I perform. Thy will be done, amen.

One of S.'s cousins calls me. He's someone I had met only briefly, much earlier. We had dined together one evening, then I never heard from him again. He learned of the tragedy and gives me a call.

He wants to know what happened.

I tell him.

He wants to know how it happened.

I tell him.

He wants to know every detail. What was he like. In what condition did I find him. What did I do. Who did I call. How did I feel.

It's not a conversation; it's an interrogation. He asks me unpleasant, morbid questions. He wants to stick the knife in and turn it around.

I let him. I answer everything.

He wants to know what I told the family. He wants to know if I went to the morgue. He wants to know what the other tenants thought.

I answer those questions, too.

In a brief resurgence of rationality, a part of me realizes that this conversation makes no sense. That it's unseemly, sick. That no one—especially someone I barely know, like him—has the right to carry on that way against a person in mourning. But I don't have the energy to fight back. I let him pursue his investigation, pervert that he is. I second his every request. I'm in such bad shape that nothing can make me feel worse. This is already the far end of the abyss. Beyond this there's nothing, no matter how much lower people try to push me.

Then at a certain point he stops. He's run out of questions. He says goodbye, as if he'd only called to chat about the weather.

Ciao.

Ciao.

No matter how hard you try to avoid it, for mourning there is a type of socializing which you have to perform.

People question you, converse with you, want to hear what happened from your mouth—and it's you they think they are consoling.

It becomes a full-time job. The acquaintances, the friends. The phone calls in the early morning, at lunchtime, late at night. I just heard. It's awful. I'm speechless. How are you?

When you lose someone, that absence becomes one of your defining characteristics. During the first few days in particular it becomes your whole identity. It becomes you.

At the beginning you are incapable, you let a family member answer for you, but then, at a certain point, it's your turn. You can't hide forever. You can't keep the world from finding you.

Sometimes I would slide into a bubble of oblivion, lose myself by watching something on television, listening to my family's conversations as they talk about ordinary little things, moments when the thought of his death fades away. And then, all of a sudden, the telephone would ring. It was me whom they were calling, there was no need to ask. That sound would tear me away from unconsciousness and plunge me back into reality.

Their intentions are noble, they want you to feel affection, closeness, but for you even this is an effort.

And that unexpressed question, which no one asks but that you perceive, inescapably, between the lines: Why did he do it?

The only true question, the one that you yourself can never answer.

Addressing the ghost of that question with other people will become a constant in your life. Your job.

After we'd been seeing each other for a couple of years, we moved in together. It's nothing we had planned. We hadn't even talked about it.

I had a studio apartment in Milan; he lived with his mother in the suburbs. He'd come to see me at night, two or three times a week, which turned into six or seven, and my apartment was too small for the two of us. Might as well accept the reality of the situation.

One night after dinner, in our new two-room sublet, we were watching something on TV, I don't remember what, when S. turned to me and said, "You know, I never would have believed I could be so happy."

He left me speechless.

He wasn't the kind of guy who talked about his feelings. I realized that this declaration had come to him spontaneously while contemplating our very normal life as a couple: barefoot, sitting on an Ikea sofa that we'd bought on sale, watching a funny show on broadcast TV.

Without his going into more detail, I could sense the deeper meaning of what he wanted to say: that this ordinary tranquility was an achievement that for years he couldn't even allow himself to imagine.

Having grown up in an environment in which homosexuality was simply inconceivable, he ignored his own nature for years, following the plan that society had laid out for him: He got married, created a family, like his brothers, his friends, like everybody around him. Then, when his marriage failed and he separated, an adult by now and free once again, he realized that he had to listen to the stirrings that he had resisted for years and years. He had his first experiences, and even had a couple of flings. Then I came along. And then came living together.

Now the pieces of the puzzle of his life, maybe for the first time, were starting to fit together. He had a son, whom he loved more than anything in the world and with whom he spent a lot of time. Hometown friends in the dark about his new life but with whom he still hung out, comfortably, thanks to a lie or two. And a partner with whom he shared an intimacy that he'd always assumed would be unavailable to him, since it was so far beyond his reach.

He had believed that certain things were not destined for him. And instead, here we were.

So despite our obvious differences, in background and personality, despite the tight finances, despite the fact that things later took another turn, for a few years we were very happy together. We really were.

We also laughed a lot. It takes an effort for me to remember this because (for years) every time that I think of him now, he is associated with suffering. The truth is that we had a lot of fun, in that period that seems so remote, me in my twenties: ancient history.

S. had a way of laughing in which his whole face participated. His eyes became two slits, his thin lips disappeared and put his teeth on display.

I know it sounds absurd, but when I think of him laughing, I see him in black and white. The first picture that I took of him is in black and white: He's lying on the sofa with his arms behind his head, laughing as he looks at the camera (at me, standing over him). An analog picture, on black-and-white film.

He had his own brand of irony. I remember once, after watching the film *Dances with Wolves* on TV, he went around for weeks speaking a made-up Sioux language, giving (unrepeatable) names to some of our habits, and making me laugh till I cried.

He loved making me laugh, even with silly pranks, like suddenly popping out from behind a door, or pulling away a chair when I was about to sit down. Joyful and childish gestures that delighted me every single time since they caught me off guard.

An adult, a manual laborer, a father.

This, too, is intimacy: the unexpected side of a person which others cannot even imagine, which belongs to you alone.

As I write these pages, I discover that it is never raining in my memories of S. Only one image is related to bad weather (the car sheltered under the roof while a storm rages outside), apart from which I only manage to remember sunsets, pebble beaches, a river running, evenings sitting on the balcony with neighbors, motorcycle trips in the mountains, a protest march on a sweltering hot day, the coolness of the air-conditioning when we went back to the hotel, snapshots of a vacation by the seaside. Every single image is clear and bright.

I wonder about this climate-revision phenomenon, having never found a comparable reference to it in anything I've read. Is this something imagined by my subconscious? A defense mechanism based on favorable meteorological conditions? Whatever it is, I'm not convinced. The naïve equation that *fair weather* = *serenity* is as phony as a three-dollar bill. I'm cognizant of the difficulties and clashes we had, the tempests that characterized our emotional life. Yet despite this awareness, there's nothing I can do: My mind is full of slightly overexposed images with saturated color. An endless summer to counter the gelid winter that came after.

Why did he do it?

In the two years before his death, S. had shown signs of growing distress, accompanied by outrageous gestures, provocations, angry outbursts, and irrational behavior.

He left his job as a truck driver all of a sudden. One night he came home and told me that he had quit. He claimed that the truck he drove was too old and hard to maneuver. That they made him work in unacceptable conditions. That they exploited him.

He said that a friend had promised him a position as a stocker at a supermarket, a sure thing. Instead there was nothing sure about it and he didn't get the job.

This triggered an endless cycle of precarious jobs, lasting anywhere from one month to three days.

He started to drink, heavily.

And to not come home at night. I didn't know where he was or what he was doing. Sometimes he drank so heavily that, like a bad joke, he couldn't find the door to our place or insert the right key. He would call a couple of wrong numbers before finding mine in his contact list. He would wake me in the dead of night to open the door.

He said that he continued to take care of child support, when in reality he was skipping the monthly payments.

By then our relationship was obviously on the rocks. He seemed to be sabotaging his entire life. Deliberately.

The ordinary happiness that had moved him so deeply was no longer enough. Once he even told me as much, in a sentence that I found equal parts extreme and senseless: "I realized that after this, there's nothing left for me in life." As if to say that something was gnawing away at him, an anxiety he'd kept at bay through a series of achievements and which was starting to get the upper hand. As if he had burned his way through life and had nothing left in reserve. A hunger he could no longer sate.

When S. took his life, he and I were not together.

Officially we had been separated for three months.

During that period we saw each other every now and then. He still had keys to the apartment, but it was in my name, and to be honest, he hadn't paid his share of the rent for God knows how long.

Sometimes he would stop by to pick up a few things he had left or to drop off others, until he found new accommodations. I could have asked for the keys back, and deprived him of the freedom to come and go as he pleased. But it seemed cruel, so I didn't. Despite the quarrels and tensions between us, he respected my privacy. He stopped by when I was at work, or he notified me that he was coming over if he knew I was home.

I've asked myself a hundred times what would have happened if I had taken back the keys.

Where would he have done it? Would he have done it in the same way or would he have used another method? Without this practical possibility, would he have had to go about things differently, and require more time? And in that longer interval, would he have had second thoughts?

My head is filled with questions that no one can ever answer.

But I am convinced that he came back here to kill himself because for him it was still home.

After all these years, I can't decide whether to be consoled or horrified by this thought.

I like listening to the music of little-known artists, always on the lookout for groups that are light-years away from radio favorites or high on the charts.

In the early 2000s I was enthusiastic about the CD *The Young Machines*, by the American indie group Her Space Holiday, which I knew almost nothing about.

When I really like an album, I try to hunt down all of the artist's other works. When I googled Her Space Holiday, I discovered that they had a previous album, but when I found it online, I was in for a shock: The title was *Home Is Where You Hang Yourself.* I couldn't complete the order. I was in the newsroom of the radio station where I worked at the time, and I remember quickly closing the page, as if I had accidentally landed on a porn site.

I later found out that Her Space Holiday was actually a single musician and, in a disturbing trick of fate, he had almost the same name as me, Marc Bianchi.

In the next few days I tried to be more rational, to tell myself that I shouldn't be so scared of a title, that I shouldn't allow those words to block me, although they were dangerously close to my experience. Making a concerted effort, I went back online and bought it. When the CD arrived, I put it on my CD shelf next to the others by the same group.

The truth? I have never listened to it. Not once.

We had been separated for three months, but this bureaucratic detail did not affect my grief.

What did it matter if our relationship had just ended or was ongoing?

S. had been my daily life for more than seven years. For such a long time that I now found it impossible to accept that I could no longer see him, hear from him, call him, touch him, fight with him, speak with him.

The fact that we had split up a few months earlier didn't change anything.

On the contrary, his sudden death had almost erased the squabbles and fights we'd been having recently. Acting as a censor, sly and meticulous, death had deleted the negative memories and saved only the ones associated with happiness. Sequences of our life as a couple were constantly coming back to me: dinners on the balcony, vacations, motorcycle rides, moves, a montage of images on an endless loop, like a Hollywood rom-com starring the two of us, happy.

In a way, his passing made me fall in love with him again.

Yet another cute trick of my unconscious, making my grief even more unbearable.

The paramedics, after certifying the death, place the corpse on the stretcher and carry it outside. They tell me which hospital they are taking him to and I nod, but I forget immediately (I have to get the information from the doorman).

I am left alone in the apartment. More alone than I have ever been before. A form of cosmic abandonment.

With that sliver of reason still left, I call S.'s sister to tell her. "He really did it," I say.

I let her absorb the information, while she passes from shock to tears. I am unable to stay on the line very long. I ask her to please tell the rest of the family and I hang up.

Then I call my parents.

I don't know what words to use, how to relate this form of the unspeakable. I ask them to come pick me up.

At that point I stop, there's nothing more I can do.

I position myself in a corner of the bedroom, almost as if I wanted to hide, huddled on the floor, my arms around my bent legs, my head on my knees, and I wait.

I am a child again.

Mama, Papa, come get me.

Come take care of me.

I regress to infancy, when I was afraid of the dark and had no idea how scary the dark really was.

I'm afraid. Come get me. Tell me that it's just a bad dream.

That it will all be over.

The words tumble out of my mouth almost incomprehensibly.

A friend insists that I see this psychic she knows. I've never believed in things like that, but I never imagined that anyone could feel as awful as I do now. Grief has made me more gullible. I'm ready to believe in wizards, angels, life after death, aliens, divine mercy, the future, the light at the end of the tunnel—anything that might offer some form of relief. That would light a match, any match, in the darkness.

My friend swears that this psychic is unlike the others. That she is "very powerful."

Okay, we'll go.

The appointment is at two thirty in the afternoon. My friend decides to go with me.

A 1950s building in an area close to the city center. The elevator has wood-framed glass doors and a little seat upholstered in threadbare velvet.

Inside the apartment my chaperone moves with the assurance of a regular. She crosses the hall, has a seat on the sofa in a small room, and gestures for me to sit next to her.

"She will call you," my friend explains.

And she does. A couple of minutes later, from the door opposite us, which was open a crack, a voice says, "Come in!"

With a nudge of her elbow my friend directs me to stand up.

I go in.

The room is dimly lit. A woman with a serene aura is seated behind a desk. A full head of white hair, a grandmotherly smile. An image that doesn't quite match the adjective "powerful" that had persuaded me to see her.

I don't know whether to feel disappointed or reassured. I suspend judgment, as I've been doing for weeks, over everything.

I sit down in front of her.

She gets straight to the point and asks why I'm there.

As I'm speaking, she holds a pendulum in her hand, pointed at the center of her desk, and lets it swing slowly back and forth.

"Do you want to know if he's all right? If he's found the light?"

"Yes."

I'm startled when she suddenly opens her hand. The pendulum falls on the desk, dragging the long chain down with it.

"If that's all you wanted, then we're already done here," she says. "From the moment you came in I could immediately sense that the man you are talking about is in the light. I could see it clearly."

I feel a sudden warmth filling my chest. S. is fine, I tell myself. He's good.

"He's all right? Are you sure?"

"He's happy, now he has found peace," she declares. "Is this all you wanted to know?"

"Yes."

"Then you can go now."

For some reason, I see the psychic's efficiency as a sign of honesty. If she were a charlatan, she would have dragged the matter out and been more dramatic. Instead she doesn't seem in the least bit concerned by the impression that her manner might create. She is frank, direct, gets right to the point because she sees no need to beat around the bush.

"If you'd like to make a donation, you can leave it there," she points to the right side of her desk. "You don't have to," she adds.

I stand up. My friend had instructed me to leave at least fifty thousand liras. I stick my hand in my pocket and fish out the banknote. I place it in the basket. She is looking away. I could have left her a five or five hundred, it wouldn't have made any difference.

I say goodbye and leave.

The clock in the waiting room tells me that the session lasted ten minutes.

The sense of relief—enormous—that I felt the moment she told me that S. was in the light is already fading: a lot less powerful than it was a few seconds ago.

My friend asks me how it went.

I attempt a smile. "She told me that S. is happy. That he's in the light now."

She gives me a hug. "I told you she was extraordinary."

Yes, she really was. Extraordinary at telling me the one thing I wanted to hear, and with magisterial certainty. Extraordinary in the way she told it.

Every fiber in my body longs for her to be right. So that my sense of relief will become permanent. And her words will be the miraculous balm that will save me. But I already know this won't be the case.

We leave the psychic's studio, take the old-fashioned elevator down, and go back out to the street. I say goodbye to my friend with another hug and walk away.

S. is in the light. Maybe.

And I will remain immersed in darkness.

I remember seeing a short movie at a film festival about a young woman who followed a stranger around town. She waited for him outside his office, stalked him as he went into a café, sat behind him on the bus. She was discreet, persistent. She made no attempt to speak to the man, who for his part did not seem to know her and ignored her presence. It was only toward the end of the film that the audience learned the secret that bound the two of them: The man had received a transplant, the heart of the woman's husband, who had died in a car accident. She followed the stranger because inside of him was the essence, still beating, of her departed love.

At the time I thought the film was poetic but manipulative, a contrived metaphor about love surviving after death.

I was naïve. I knew nothing about life and grief.

If after the death of S. I could have followed his heart in a stranger, I would have spent my days going everywhere with him.

In the eyes of others, S. and I were an odd couple.

Being with someone so different creates more difficulties outside of the couple than inside. You have to constantly negotiate the differences that others might notice and that your everyday life together have smoothed over.

In our respective circles, we took turns being the fish out of water: He had little in common with mine; I had almost nothing in common with his.

We didn't talk about it much. We knew that this was the way things were going to be and we lived with it. It was part of what made being together so appealing. A dual challenge to convention.

We were a mixed couple, but of the same ethnicity and sex.

S.'s manners were brusque and direct, which was his MO but which others sometimes saw as inappropriate if not downright rude. Once we went to the Linate airport together to pick up my friend Gianmarco, who was living abroad and I hadn't seen for months. This was the first time he met S., whom he had only heard about in my letters. In the car, the two of us started talking like mad, as if we were anxious to make up for the long interval that had separated us. S. was driving, minding the road, not our conversation. At one point, without warning, he pulled over next to a roadside bar and announced, "I'm in the mood for a beer, what about you guys?" Taken by surprise, we both shook our heads. "Okay, ten minutes then," he said and got out. I was used to his straightforward manner, so I didn't pay him any mind. Gianmarco, on the other hand, who was coming from Paris, where he frequented a milieu of stylists and designers, and was probably more accustomed to disco parties with champagne and cocaine than to roadside bars in the afternoon, gave me a worried look. "Is he always so bossy?" he asked. "Look, if he's violent, you'd better tell me. Does he beat you?"

I burst out laughing. S. was a gentle and affectionate lover. The very idea that he would get physical was ridiculous, even comical, but others might see his rough exterior as an indication of something more dangerous, I needed to be aware of that. There were, of course, other examples that illustrated the opposite.

During a weekend in Rome we were invited to dinner, along with half a dozen other people, by a friend of mine, an established writer, a finalist for Italy's top literary award, the Strega, a man whose name was fashionable in both cultural and political spheres. He had recently moved to the Monti neighborhood and wanted to give us a tour of his new apartment. We passed through rooms with frescoed high ceilings, bookshelves that took up entire walls. The hallways were filled with paintings by contemporary artists.

During our tour S. lit a cigarette without asking. Our host glowered at him and told him to smoke on the balcony. This reprimand also seemed directed at me, by association, but I pretended not to notice, feigning indifference to this faint diplomatic incident. I let S. finish his cigarette alone, while he looked out over the panorama of Roman terraces.

A few minutes later, over drinks, our host apologized for the lack of hot water in the house, explaining that the boiler was broken and the repairman who had promised to come by that day had postponed the appointment until the next morning. While we were sipping our drinks, S. got up from his chair and asked if our host could show him where the system was located. Our host led him to the kitchen, where I overheard S. asking, "Any chance you have a screwdriver?"

Fifteen minutes later the boiler was working, and the famous writer looked upon my companion with the admiration normally reserved for misunderstood geniuses.

Now I basked in the praise that sentimental proximity had earned me. Meanwhile S. had gone back to his cocktail, as indifferent to praise as he had been to the earlier reprimand.

For S. social conventions had never been a priority.

I had to empty out his closets. Give away his stuff. I don't remember what I did with it, whether I gave it to a family member or to charity. It's another one of those gaps in my memory that riddle this story. Who got his clothes? I don't know. The baseball caps, the belts, the T-shirts? What about his CDs? And his car, did someone come by to pick it up and take it away? I don't know, these questions all belong to a broad swath of memories from that period that my mind has decided to erase.

What I did keep were his hair clippers, since we both used them and I knew I still would. I wondered whether I should. They weren't the ordinary kind, they were a professional model he had ordered from a hair salon supplier, meant for a barber, with detachable blades of different lengths. He bought them because he liked his hair cut really short and felt there was no point in paying a hairdresser for a buzz cut; he might as well do it himself. With time he converted me to a military cut, too. He used the shorter blade, the 0.01, I used an intermediate size, the 0.03, which cut my hair short but, unlike him, left something on the nape of my neck.

If it had been a regular model, I'm sure I would have given it away, along with the rest of his things, but I didn't know where to buy professional clippers, so I held on to them.

The only clothes I kept were a sweater and a pair of jeans. The sweater because it still had his scent. I noticed when I was about to pack it up. A sensory trace of him, imprisoned in the fibers. I held it to my nose and sniffed for days on end. At night, before going to bed. During the day, when the grief became excruciating. A single gesture to fight the madness that had me in its grip. I would open the closet and reach for the folded sweater, which was lying on a shelf at eye level. I would reach for it, bring it toward me, bury my face in it, and breathe in. In that moment S. would still be there with me. I could feel him. I tried not to overindulge: That scent was a treasure to be savored, to be preserved. I would put the sweater back in its place, close the closet, and be careful not to reopen it too often.

As the days went by, however, the scent grew fainter until it disappeared altogether.

I knew it would happen; it was inevitable.

That scent was a fading echo, one of the myriad traces that he had left in my life which he was now taking away with him.

Our separation was interminable, infinite subtleties in saying farewell.

I'm not sure why I kept his jeans. Because they were his trademark, I guess. He only wore jeans, and didn't buy any other type of trouser. If you asked him why, he would answer that he was a jeans guy, period.

Years later, during a move, someone packed them in a box with other stuff. When I opened the box, I realized I could no longer recognize them. It was a popular model, I had similar ones myself. Which were his? Which were mine?

As a teenager, the first novel I read that mentioned homosexuality had a scene in which two boys, after making love for the first time, were no longer able to tell whose white briefs were lying at the foot of the bed, since they both wore the same kind. Their uncertainty showed how much their identities had already merged.

For me, time has erased the symbolic value of that fetish, and evaporated that memory like perfume.

For seven years we had been one.

It would be pointless nowadays to try to distinguish between my jeans and his old pair.

His sister asked me for a photo of S. to affix to the gravestone.

I was the only person who had recent pictures.

I chose one where he was flashing his best smile.

He is wearing a leather biker jacket. His head is shaved and he has a salt-and-pepper goatee. He is smiling happily at the camera. At me.

I don't know which trip it was. I remember taking it the minute we arrived. S. had just parked his bike and was turning around. He didn't know that I was taking his picture. When he saw the camera pointed at him, he smiled, more out of surprise than anything else.

I know he was happy. On motorcycle trips he always was.

Elena agreed that it was his best picture, and the most appropriate. Because in that shot "he was himself."

She took it to the undertaker for the ceramic photo to be affixed to the gravestone. All the details of the funeral were handled by the family. The first time I went to the cemetery, I was in for a shock. In the photo, rather than a goatee, S. had a dark black mustache. S. hated mustaches.

I immediately phoned Elena. "They made a mistake when they touched up the photo," she explained, "but it was too late to redo it."

The picture of S., the one by which he would be seen and remembered from now on, does not represent him and has no connection to reality.

He never wore a mustache; now he is sporting one, smiling for eternity.

That night, after I found the body, after my brain had registered what had happened and tried to turn it into a concept I could absorb, understand, and react to, after I tried to scream and no voice came out, after I circled the room like a robot gone haywire, unable to do anything except fold in on myself in search of a way out, an explanation, a switch to turn off the nightmare I was living, I went out on the balcony and started to scream toward the courtyard, toward the stairwell.

Help. Help. Help.

I don't know who I was addressing, who I was begging for help. The whole world.

A few minutes later someone arrives. Three men. People from the building whom I've never met but I recognize, having seen them on the stairs or in the lobby.

I point toward the interior of the apartment. They enter, I follow.

I see the bewilderment on their faces, the horror. Then clarity starts to prevail. Two of them hold up S.'s body, while the third looks around the kitchen until he spots the metal cutlery rack above the sink. He grabs a knife and goes back to the others to sever the rope. They look almost as if they know what to do, as if it has happened before, as if each person's DNA was inscribed with instructions on how to react to a situation like this.

They lay the corpse on the ground in silence.

They look at me as if to say there is no more they can do (and in fact, there isn't), then they leave.

The door is still open.

On the landing I can sense silhouettes and voices. Other neighbors, people drawn by my screams, wanting to know, to understand. I hear them whispering about what to do. No one else walks in; it's just me and the body of S. until the paramedics arrive.

In the months that followed, I ran into the three men from time to time. By the main door, on the stairs with their wives, in the yard as they stored the children's bicycles in the rack, in the doorman's office picking up the mail. We exchanged glances, always in silence.

I wondered what I could say to them. To thank them would be grotesque. Do you thank somebody for a thing like that? No. There are no appropriate formulas, no applicable conventions.

Only once did one of them decide to speak. I was in the elevator. He held the doors before they closed and came in with his two children. Only then did he realize it was me. Maybe he would have waited for the next one if he had known.

One of the sons was holding a DVD from a rental chain. The father noticed that I was staring at the blue-and-yellow packaging.

"We picked out a funny movie," he said. "Something to cheer us up."

"You have the right idea," I replied.

We exchanged a weak smile, pretending as hard as we could that we were ordinary neighbors.

To have shared the most tragic moment in my life with three strangers is absurd, but indelible (for me, for them). But in some way it will unite us forever, even if we didn't know how to put it into words.

> **"Sometimes** being offered tenderness feels like the very proof that you've been ruined."
> —OCEAN VUONG,
> *ON EARTH WE'RE BRIEFLY GORGEOUS*

My search for a panacea led me to make an appointment with a pranotherapist in Rome. Some friends told me about her. They say she gives treatments that you can't explain. That yes, she does give you a massage, but as she does, she transmits her energy to you, and understands what is going on deep inside. She is able to help you. To provide you with answers.

A friend of my sister, a university professor who has been a client for years, makes a personal commitment to be my liaison, to find a slot for me in the woman's busy schedule.

On the day of our appointment, I wake up with a temperature. I can't get out of bed, much less take a train and travel for four and a half hours. I call the woman on her cell phone and explain the situation. I am mortified because I know she was doing me a favor by agreeing to see me on such short notice. She sounds calm on the other end and reschedules my appointment for the following week. I thank her and apologize profusely, as if I were on the line with Joaquín Navarro-Valls, the pope's press secretary, for an appointment with the Holy Father. I'm not myself. Because of my temperature, because of my prolonged inner exhaustion.

The next week I go in.

Her studio looks like a doctor's office. In the waiting room there are a few chairs and a low table with newspapers and magazines. On the wall are posters of cherry trees in bloom, waterfalls, and Alpine landscapes. Standard depictions of bucolic serenity.

When the door to her study opens, I discover that she is short in stature with medium-length black hair and a round face. The physique of an innkeeper or a baker. An image more carnal than spiritual.

Energy makes curious choices when it channels itself into the material world.

She tells me to take off my shoes and sweater, and makes me lie down on the cot, flat on my stomach.

She starts to massage me, gently, beginning with my legs. As she does so, she asks me why I'm there. What is my story, my malaise.

For the millionth time I describe what happened, giving a performance that sounds like a broken record, in a desperate attempt to find relief. Wherever I might be, and with whomever I happen to find myself.

I don't really know what pranotherapy is, or how it works. I don't even know whether I believe in it. I'm incapable of absorbing this information, of analyzing it according to intellectual categories or metaphysical beliefs. In the past few months my analytical abilities have been suspended. Nothing makes sense. Everything makes sense. Do with me what you will.

She continues to massage me.

I wonder when the contact between us will take place. When her hands will start to transmit to me that warmth, that redemptive energy whose praises my friends have sung.

I feel cold. Cold everywhere. Cold in her hands, cold in my benumbed heart.

For a while I let her continue. Then I ask, "Do you feel anything?"

I don't really know what I mean, I don't know if there is an answer to this question.

She says, "You are in great pain. It's very difficult to enter into contact with you."

I know. Thank you. I could have told you that myself.

The session continues for a while longer, but it's clearly not working the way it's supposed to.

I feel no energy radiating from her hands.

She's manipulating a disjointed mannequin. My muscles are relaxed, my spirit is a block of ice.

As I'm getting dressed, she says, "I'm sorry."

She realizes that she has failed.

I am not as upset as she is. I know that no one can save me. She tried, but the monster devouring me cannot be confronted with bare hands.

There is one thing I have to do in the days after the funeral, which is to talk to his son. He's still a kid, and the impact this event has had on him must be devastating.

I call him one evening and ask if I can come by to see him.

He answers yes, with the awkwardness of a teenager who doesn't understand adults and their ridiculous requests.

We arrange to meet on Saturday afternoon.

At the house I am greeted by his mother, the ex-wife of S. Today she seems calm and friendly. She asks if I'd like a coffee, and I say no thank you because my stomach is knotted with tension and all the other things that are happening, so I have a more innocuous glass of water while she goes to call her son.

David is in his room with headphones on, a typical teenager. With a frail and hesitant manner, he comes to the kitchen table where I am sitting.

"Want to go for a ride?" I ask.

He looks at his mother. "Are you coming, too?" His is not so much a question as a plea. But Angela understands.

"No, it's better if you two talk alone."

We get into the car and I start the engine. I decide to head for the edge of town, where the factories and warehouses are located. I pull into the empty parking lot of a factory. It is closed, we have the whole parking lot to ourselves. I turn off the engine. A light fog surrounds us. The desolation of the place and the chill of December complete the picture.

We couldn't be more miserable. The time has come for me to speak.

"Do you know why I wanted to see you?"

David shrugs his shoulders. "Because you're sorry that my dad died," he says, but he says it like he doesn't mean it, like someone taking a random stab at an answer.

Today he seems more childlike than usual.

He is in that limbo, that age before you become somebody. Delicate bones, the first signs of peach fuzz on the upper lip, the elongated body. No longer a child, not yet a man. A creature in transit.

I am reminded of an afternoon from the previous summer. He had come to see S. and we went to a municipal pool, all three of us. There was a newsstand next to the entrance.

S. asked him if he wanted something to read. David looked for a while at the newspapers on display, then chose a puppet inside a cellophane bag. A product clearly meant for younger kids. S. was surprised but said nothing. He took a magazine for himself and paid.

As we entered the pool area, David was clearly embarrassed by his purchase, but he hadn't been able to resist. A hiccup of childhood, which was still legitimate in this transitional phase.

I don't know why I am remembering this now. Maybe because in those days of heartbreak, all he needed was to be consoled, to be hugged. He has reverted to being more of a puppy than ever, seeking protection.

What I am about to say will not be easy.

"I wanted to talk to you about what happened," I say. "To know what you think."

"I don't think anything," he answers immediately, defensive.

"You know your father loved you, don't you?"

I see his facial muscles stiffen, his expression become harder. The embers simmer beneath the ashes.

"You do know, don't you?" I insist.

At that point he blurts out, "If he did love me then why did he do it, huh? Why didn't he think of me?"

"He never stopped thinking about you."

"That's not true, he was a coward."

"He was the opposite. How often did he usually phone you?"

"Every night."

"And in the ten days before he killed himself, how many times did he call you?"

"Never."

"Do you understand why?"

David is silent.

"Because he couldn't. With everyone else he could pretend, but not with you. He wouldn't have been able to hear your voice and pretend. You were too important to him."

It starts to get dark outside. The contours of the world melt into the fog, as if there were nothing else in the universe besides this microscopic space, the warm interior of a car with the two of us inside. My voice and the breathing of the boy.

"At the times when we were happiest, he would always say the same thing: 'You are the second most beautiful thing in my life.' Do you know what the first one was?"

David looks at me, realizing that my question is rhetorical.

"It was you. He also used to say, 'I've made many mistakes in life, but there's at least one thing I did right.'"

David's silence gives me implicit permission to continue.

"We can never know the depth of the pain he had inside that drove him to kill himself. But we do know why he stopped calling you in those final days. He had decided to end it all, and you were the only thing that still tied him to life."

David begins to cry. Two big tears roll down his cheeks that he cannot and will not hold back.

I look away, shifting my gaze to the empty space surrounding us. I respect his emotional state, and let him know that it's all right to let it out.

For a couple of minutes we remain like this, suspended in an emotional silence.

He is the one who breaks the silence. "Thank you. Now I understand why you wanted to see me," he says. He looks up and adds: "In the past few days I couldn't stop thinking that my dad did what he did because he didn't care about me. But you made me see the opposite: that he really did love me."

This time I am the one who is moved. What he has just said is so much more than I would have expected from a teenager.

In the wasteland of this absurd grief enveloping me, where nothing seems to make sense, I still managed to do one good thing: I returned a father to a son.

Grief lies in wait for me, ambushes me when I least expect it. Lately it's started to do so more frequently and in the most inopportune places, at random moments, with a brutal and unstoppable rapidity.

A typical scene: I am at the agency, on the landing of the stairs between floors, coming back from a meeting. I'm suddenly jolted by a flash of awareness: an intrusive, cannibalistic thought that I'd been trying to ward off by focusing on deadlines, office hours, errands, and society's demand for productivity.

The mechanism is hard to explain: It's as if my mind set aside one concept for a while and stopped dealing with it; but then it's back to being the focus of my thoughts again, demanding its rightful place, virulently, placing itself implacably before everything and erasing the rest. It happens rapidly, like a slap in the face.

I remain on the stairs, gasping for air. Tears come to my eyes, they become a river. I start to sob; my legs give way and I slump to the steps. I lose control and yield to crying my heart out, in a wail that becomes a whimper.

Maybe fate will be kind to me. For a few minutes the stairs might be deserted. People don't need to go from one floor to another so frequently. Plus there's the elevator. It wouldn't hurt to have a solitary interlude, to spare me any embarrassment.

But instead.

I hear footsteps approaching but I can't react: stop crying, stand up, run. I no longer have the ability, not at moments like this. I remain there, come what may.

My agency is owned by three partners: two creatives and one administrator. The creatives, Number One and Number Two, I deal with every day, so we are close by virtue of our constantly meeting on a professional basis. Number Three I see passing by now and then, but I hardly ever speak with him: I'm not even sure he knows my name.

And who should pass me on the stairs but Number Three. Imagine the scene: me sobbing, curled into a ball; him climbing the stairs quickly, a document in one hand, an attitude that emanates urgency.

He sees me and freezes: How is one supposed to behave in such a situation?

What does a man do when faced by another man in despair? Or a boss seeing one of his employees?

Are there rules for these circumstances?

We exchange a simple glance. I don't know how, but the message gets through.

Number Three says nothing, does nothing. He keeps going, steps past me, and continues on his way.

I continue to wallow in my tears, immensely grateful to have been ignored.

Five months later.

It's spring. A little party is thrown at the agency. A celebration for having won an important project, with an international client and a budget that is remarkable by Italian standards. The partners can't hide their satisfaction.

Lately I'm doing much better in public. I've learned how to manage depression in private, how to avoid bursting into tears in front of strangers and friends, how to be sociable when I need to be.

Like today.

I'm surrounded by colleagues holding glasses of spumante. They laugh, they drink. I drink, too. I smile.

Number One made some opening remarks, congratulated the entire agency, and then proposed a toast. Half an hour of alcohol-fueled conversation before we all go home.

In that moment of general serenity, of corporate cheer, something wild happens. Number Three crosses the room, comes up to me, and, in front of everyone, gives me a hug. A real hug, not a pat on the back. An affectionate hug, as if we were friends who hadn't seen each other in years, two reunited brothers. A hug that astonishes everyone who sees it.

Number Three is our most reserved, most distant partner, the one we creatives know the least. For him to get close to any of us is rare. For him to give a hug is inconceivable.

We are making a spectacle of ourselves.

For a while now I've been immune to how people

react to me in public, to the curiosity aroused by my grief. Yet I cannot deny that this leaves me dumbfounded.

As he hugs me, Number Three says, "I'm glad to see you're doing a little better."

He doesn't need to add anything. I understand.

It is not a corporate hug, and it has nothing to do with a celebration among colleagues, with congratulations. It is an imploded hug, the reaction he withheld on the day that he passed me on the stairs. A gesture that waited months before coming into being, before becoming concrete.

Human compassion has a timetable. Sometimes you have to respect it.

And he did.

(**I later found** out that an ambitious colleague, mistaking that hug for an open expression of professional appreciation, and fearing, God forbid, that I might be getting a promotion, a shot at a major advancement, went and told him that I was interviewing all over town in order to leave the agency. An outright lie. An attempt to discredit me. So gratuitous and petty that I react to it immediately. I go directly to Number Three's office and tell him that the rumor is completely unfounded. That I am not looking to transfer. That at this moment in my life it would be absurd to even think I have the bandwidth to be seeking new employment. He thanks me for the explanation, admitting that he, too, had found the rumor unlikely. As for my malicious colleague, I hold nothing against him. I can't deal with confrontation. To me a fight over issues in the workplace would be meaningless. All my energies are directed elsewhere: They're focused on survival.)

I try to remember what it was like to be alone in that apartment again on that first night back.

In the days following the tragedy, I went to my parents' and stayed with them for a week or so. After the funeral I returned to work and a couple of days later to the apartment. Alone, by choice.

But how was that first night? Did I sleep? Did I stay awake staring into darkness with my eyes wide open and anxiety in my chest? Did I cry, did I scream? Was I resigned, peaceful?

I swear I don't remember. That, too, I have erased. It's strange how our memory reacts to a shock: Some images remain indelible, others are wiped away, for no apparent reason. A puzzle in which the figures have vivid coloring but entire areas are missing.

To remember that period is to excavate the ground in search of buried civilizations: So much has been lost.

On this ripped tapestry, a haphazard weave of holes and clear memories, and a final design that will never be complete, I have two sharp recollections of the day S. died.

The first: As I was shouting "Help" on the stairs, one thought went through my mind. This is the most painful moment of your life, I said to myself. A moment of clarity: Whatever else might happen, nothing will ever compare to this.

(Absurd how our mind can insert such a sharp thought in a moment when our awareness is shattered.)

The second: When the men who laid S. on the ground went out, leaving me alone with the corpse, I got down on my knees and touched him. I stroked his face. It was cold. Or maybe not, maybe the perception wasn't thermal: I could sense that he was lifeless.

S. is no longer here, I thought. S. is no longer in this body. In movies, TV series, and news reports from scenes of a bombing, we are always seeing grief-stricken relatives who cannot tear themselves away from the body of their loved one. For one last time they touch him, hold him, and kiss him on the forehead, on the lips. They want to prolong this closeness, this last possible moment together.

I did not feel any of that. I stood up and went to the other room. It already made no sense to be next to him.

This I remember distinctly.

The certainty that I had already lost him forever, and in his place were only the remains.

A shell.

S. was no longer there.

("When you get back, I'll be gone.")

I'm writing this book in fragments because fragments are all that I have.

Maybe I should call them shards—consistent with the earlier metaphor of buried civilizations—or artifacts.

Things that are shattered, whatever we decide to call them.

When I write I modify some details. I change the order in which things happened. I shift around the dates of people and things. I followed the same approach in my earlier memoirs. What interests me is the truth, not a word-for-word correspondence to reality. I have always thought of truth and reality as two separate concepts: When you write you have to establish order and turn life into literature. You have to help the reader make sense of things, not copy down a series of disconnected events.

This is not a diary.

Sometimes things happened exactly as I describe them, and sometimes I alter them out of deference to the writer in me.

Whenever I've shifted the time sequence, and changed the dates or names, it's because the narrator's sensibility is more effective than the reporter's.

If someone were to ask which parts of the book are true, I would answer, without hesitation: All of them.

"The things that happen to us are true.
The stories we tell about it are writing."
—LIDIA YUKNAVITCH,
THE CHRONOLOGY OF WATER: A MEMOIR

The French musician Erik Satie began his memoir, *A Mammal's Notebook*, with this sentence: "I am called Erik Satie like anyone else."

I am called Matteo Bianchi like anyone else.

In Satie's case, the sentence was the literary hyperbole of a surrealist; in my case, a statement of fact.

Bianchi is the third most common surname in Italy. In addition, according to data I found on the Web, there is about one Matteo for every seven hundred inhabitants. The Matteo Bianchi combination is therefore pretty frequent.

When I was at university and went to the registrar's office to renew my student ID, I was twice issued the ID of a namesake instead.

When we still used to bring rolls of film to a camera shop to be developed, I would pick up my prints only to find that I'd been given another person's vacation pictures.

When someone tried to clone my credit card, the customer service representative I was speaking with introduced himself and turned out to have my same first and last name.

When I left the advertising agency where I had been working for seven years, one of the candidates who interviewed to be my replacement was named Matteo

Bianchi. He didn't get the job, maybe to avoid confusing my former colleagues and clients, but to me the risk of being replaced by someone with my same name was irrefutable proof that I was destined to be anonymous.

Once, out of sheer curiosity, I googled "Matteo Bianchi" and found all kinds of people: a journalist, a videographer, a cyclist, a children's book author, a pharmacist, a singer-songwriter, a mayor from the right-wing Lega party, a sports doctor, a scientist, a soccer player...

An army of counterfeit me's.

I quickly got used to having a name that, rather than identify me, turned me into one among many. A birth certificate that sentences me to impersonality.

One of the reasons I decided to write this book is my anonymity, which makes sense occasionally, in both symbolic and concrete terms.

It doesn't matter whether or not this is my story. Because if you have been through the same experience as I have, you will have felt the same things. You are as much Matteo Bianchi as I am. Even if our circumstances, time, ages, relationships, and sex are different, they're just details, as we all know.

I've been invited to speak at a three-day conference in Turin, an international workshop with dozens of participants. I don't know any of them, but I appreciate the circumstance of being in a totally new environment among people I've never met.

S. has been dead for six months.

At the restaurant of the hotel where the conference is being held, the seats are not assigned. At the first lunch break I find myself sharing a table with a speaker from the Netherlands, an African American man from Miami, a Canadian woman, a Belgian woman, a Brazilian woman, and another Italian, a man from Rome.

Our initial awkwardness is only momentary; we find ourselves conversing as if we were longtime friends and had known each other for years. The random way we were brought together at the same table immediately turns into a bond. We end up spending all three days together: at the conference, the lunches, the dinners, and the evenings out drinking at bars around town.

Being a stranger among strangers is comforting; there is something magical about this aura of unity created among us, destined to last for such a short time. Each of us recognizes this.

On the last night of the conference, I have an unusual dream.

I am in a giant amusement park and I wander curiously among the various rides. I go to a merry-go-round that consists of a horizontal wheel to which rows of two-seaters are attached. I decide to climb on and take a whole one for myself. The merry-go-round starts to move, slowly at first then faster, and I start to really enjoy it. Indeed, I tell myself that it's been a long time since I've been on a ride like this, and I'd forgotten how much fun it could be. The carousel is spinning at a dizzying speed now, I can't even catch a glimpse of the faces of the people in the other seats, everything is too hectic and confusing. Rather than worrying me, this insane speed makes me laugh until I cry. Then my car seat detaches from the merry-go-round and starts to shoot toward the sky. I'm not afraid, on the contrary, I'm ecstatic. I'm flying skyward, the wind in my hair, the earth receding beneath me. I am making an unpredictable journey and the sensation is amazing. In a sudden moment of rationality, I realize that I am happy, happier than I've been for months. And that's when it happens, when I hear S.'s voice by my side, whispering in my ear: "This happiness is my gift to you. Happy birthday."

I wake up with a start.

It is the morning of April 18: I had forgotten it was my birthday.

This happiness is his gift to me.

To this day it is the most beautiful dream I have ever had.

(**Despite plans and** promises with the participants in the Turin workshop, we would never see one another again. We were too far apart, and the circumstances of our first meeting were too random.

I did run into the Belgian man once, at a festival a few months later. Enough time to say hello and give each other a hug, but also to realize that the magical alchemy of before was the product of special circumstances impossible to rediscover or re-create anywhere else.

Several years later, I come to find out that the oldest member of our group, the Canadian woman, has left the field of communications to take up cooking and has published a memoir with a small press. I manage to find the book and order it from Amazon. I am surprised to find her reminisce about our week in Turin, a clear sign that for her, like the rest of us, it had been a significant and unexpected moment. The paragraph takes up little more than a page and is very affectionate. Her description of the others is realistic, but she speaks of me as "a creative middle-aged Italian." At the time I was thirty-three. I wonder why she depicts me as a fifty-year-old gentleman, but then I understand. The six months since S.'s death had been like twenty years: They had transformed me physically, made me skinnier, whitened my hair, altered my character. I had stopped being lighthearted and disorganized, and become a thoughtful man who listened a lot and preferred to smile rather than participate in the conversation, a man who kept to the sidelines of life and watched it pass by. I was an old man: Calling me middle-aged was generous on her part. This is how a foreigner from across the ocean met and remembered me.)

He left several letters behind. For his son, for his ex-wife, for his sister, for me.

He left me not only that final letter but also a notebook with dozens of letters, written over the course of the last few months. A complete farewell book.

He didn't like writing, never read novels, was all manual labor and no meditation, had penned for weeks the words that would accompany our separation.

I read that notebook only once, in the days following his suicide, then I locked it in a drawer and never touched it again, but it is the gesture for which I am most grateful to him, since it provided a justification for my survival. In its pages he wrote several times that the extreme action he was about to take was about him, about the anguish eating him up, and not about our separation.

He was absolving me.

I should pick it up again and reread his long messages of farewell, but I'm not sure I'll ever have the courage.

It would be like sticking my hand in a fire, knowing full well how badly it would burn.

Years after the tragedy, on a summer night during vacation.

I'm with a group of friends, we've rented a beachfront house on one of the Aeolian Islands.

We are having a glass of wine on the patio before going out for dinner. An argument starts over something trivial that turns unexpectedly into a quarrel. One member of the group unleashes an aggressiveness that he'd kept under control until then, showing particular animosity toward me.

I'm surprised, we've been friends for many years, he'd never shown any signs of finding me insufferable, I don't know what has gotten into him.

And then, with no connection to the issue in dispute, he decides to reveal to everyone some very personal things about me. My frailty and pettiness in the period after the suicide. Confidences I had shared from the abyss into which I'd fallen. The most intimate details of my depression blurted out in public out of spite.

I had bared myself to him, so he knows where to point the gun to hurt me. Now he's enjoying pulling the trigger.

I'm not the kind of guy that loses his temper. Even in that circumstance I say only two things.

First: You bastard.

Second: I will never forgive you for this.

I'm like that line from a popular Italian song, "*Se prometto poi mantengo*," I keep my promises. In the months to come he will try to patch things up. He'll call. He'll ask if he can see me, to explain himself.

I always answer with the same monosyllable: No.

I make him disappear forever, like in a magic trick.

(**I told you** I've become invincible, that now I have powers.)

For a few months in my early twenties, I dated a guy my age. It ended abruptly when I found out he'd been cheating on me for weeks. The moment I got wind of his infidelity, I showed up at his studio apartment to confront him. He didn't even try to feign innocence and accepted my angry outburst with muted resignation. I screamed and shed a few tears, the wounded lover, realizing that this confrontation marked the end of our relationship. In the heat of the moment, I took off my shoes and socks, and circled his room barefoot for a few minutes, only to then put them back on. It was the dead of winter, and my gesture was utterly senseless. I would probably have forgotten about it except that, a few months later, after the storm had passed and we were back to being friends on a more civil basis, he asked me for an explanation. I was suddenly reminded of what I'd done in a moment of despair and repressed immediately after. I realized that it had been a momentary suspension of reality, a brush with a small, innocent madness disgorged when my heart was broken and my mind was trying to make sense of it. A temporary blackout, a gesture devoid of logic in a circumstance where I felt I had to do something at all costs while instead there was nothing I could do.

Proof that the loss of reason is always close at hand, only one step away; that distress, panic, and pain can take the upper hand and destroy everything in a few moments.

To simply recognize this is terrifying.

Sometimes I'm afraid that this extreme pain will drive me to madness.

I'm afraid because it does occur every so often, for a few seconds. When I realize it's happening, I freeze: But what if at some point I no longer notice?

One night I'm driving back to my parents' house. I'm on my way from the city to the countryside, reassured by the familiar landscape of rice paddies and farmland around where I was raised.

I realize that I haven't seen or heard from S. in days. How come, I ask myself. Why am I letting so much time go by? As soon as I get home, I'll call him. I want to know how he's doing, figure out when we'll see each other again.

These thoughts pass through my head as I drive, amid the sparse, quiet traffic of these provincial back roads, while a flock of birds flies over cornfields set ablaze by the sunset. A strange peacefulness falls over me, the subtle joy that a positive decision has given me (I'm going home, I'm going to call him).

Then, in an instant, I am pierced by reality. Like the rending of a veil, my slumbering consciousness goes on alert again.

S. is dead.

I haven't seen him, haven't heard from him for two weeks because he's dead. How could I forget? How could my mind keep functioning for a few minutes while ignoring this truth?

I have to pull the car over and stop by the side of the road.

I'm struggling to breathe.

Nothing like this has ever happened to me before. I realize that for a short while my mind replaced the tragic reality I was living with another reality, an identical parallel world in which everything was the same except for one thing: S. was still alive.

Is this what madness is? To take for good, for *true*, a more acceptable representation of reality, for the mind to give up on truth and replace it with the closest and most innocuous form?

For a few moments this is how I felt.

Now I know what it's like.

I sit there, stunned and dismayed, trying to breathe regularly again, while a line of lazy cars glides by.

Go home, flee the madness, you who can.

Let me resume the story about the guy I was dating in my twenties. After he broke my heart, I wanted to defy death: That night, on my way back from his house, as I was driving, upset and feeling desperate, I chose not to brake at the stoplight and to go through the intersection on red.

To be honest, there was little chance of anything serious happening. It was late, and I was on a country road with no traffic. I glided through the intersection unscathed.

I don't know what I was expecting. An accident? A collision? Did I want to hurt myself or hurt the person making me suffer? Was I only trying to scare myself or did I want to feel an extreme thrill? A chaotic muddle of all the above.

In the next few days, having come to my senses, I looked back on that moment with concern but also with a certain amount of bluster. "I fucked up," I kept saying, using this harmless term (fucked up) to downplay the risk, and dismiss it as if it were a student prank.

Maybe all of us, as kids, try to challenge ourselves through acts of sheer recklessness, to test the feeling of immortality typical of youth, the riotous omnipotence that flows through our veins.

Now I remember that episode with horror, thinking how tragic it could have turned out and how careless I had been.

Maybe this, too, is what we mean by experience: a retroactive form of terror.

I found out that S. had made some wild purchases in the weeks before his suicide, including an expensive next-generation cell phone and other electronic devices. He bought them through a payment plan offered by the store.

Another sign of how determined he was to end it all: He couldn't afford those items, but he knew for certain that he would never have to pay for them.

A final sneer at capitalism.

I convince myself that individual therapy doesn't work for me. That I should try group therapy, that sharing my malaise with other people who are suffering might bring me more solace than a private session ever could.

I'm willing to try every avenue.

I search online for information and find the name of a group facilitator. I call him and ask if we can meet. He suggests a couple of times that conflict with my work schedule, then he agrees to see me during my lunch break. Coincidentally, his office is in the center of town, not far from the agency. On the day of our appointment I head out on foot, a twelve-minute walk.

The therapist is Italian, but there is something Middle Eastern about his appearance. Traces of DNA from his ancestry, I imagine. He is a handsome man, with short curly black hair and full lips, from central casting, like an actor in a TV series about doctors. He speaks in a calm, reassuring manner.

As I am explaining my situation, he never breaks eye contact. Every so often he nods his head pensively.

After telling him what I've been experiencing in recent months, I go to the heart of the matter: "I've already seen therapists, but I feel like one-on-one sessions don't work for me. It's as if nothing can touch me, nothing gets to what's bothering me deep down. Do you understand what I mean?"

"Perfectly." He flashes a professional smile.

"So I thought that maybe, I don't know, meeting with other people might work on a different emotional level..."

"I agree. Having people around you who choose to talk about their pain, their anxieties, can really help to increase the feeling of empathy, and encourage you to open up and share your burden with others."

"Is it all right if I ask what kinds of trauma the other participants in the group have experienced?"

"Oh, all kinds. Some are grieving the loss of a parent, even if the parent was elderly, others have just moved here from another city and feel ill-equipped to deal with life in a metropolis like Milan. There are women in executive positions who have to face the everyday stress that comes with the job...a really very diverse group."

The doctor seemed quite pleased with the summary he had just given me. I wasn't, and was left speechless: Adults who have lost an elderly parent and transients struggling to fit into a new environment? If these are traumas, then what would you call my issue?

I try to find the least offensive way to ask my next question.

"I realize that these can be major issues, but I'm wondering whether anyone in the group has suffered...how can I put this?...*injuries* that are similar to mine."

He indicates that he is thinking about my question for a moment, then shakes his head. "No, I would say that yours is probably the most traumatic event."

He finally catches the bewilderment etched on my face. "Oh, but you shouldn't compare. This isn't a competition to see who is suffering the most. In circumstances like these, what matters is the experience of the group. Each individual has his or her own reasons for participating in meetings, and no one trauma is more or less valid than the others. I hope you understand."

Maybe he's right. What am I turning into? A pain snob? Bragging that my tragedy is worse than yours?

"Before making up your mind, why don't you try a meeting?" he says.

I agree.

He tells me that the next session is scheduled in ten days, in this studio, at lunchtime.

"Can I count on you to be one of the participants?"

"Yes, I'd be happy to join."

The day before the session, I receive a call from him in the early afternoon at the agency.

"This is Dr. Ripamonti."

"Ah, good afternoon, Doctor."

"I was wondering why you didn't come today."

I'm surprised by his question. "But it wasn't for today," I hasten to reply, while reaching for the datebook in my backpack.

"The session was scheduled for today," he insists.

I flip through the pages, and there it is, my handwritten note. "I wrote it down in my datebook: Tuesday at one."

"It was for Monday. You wrote down the wrong day."

We both go quiet.

In psychological terms this is what is called a "Freudian slip." It's an unconscious mistake, for example, if you're afraid your wife will find out that you've been secretly drinking and you forget the bottle of whiskey on the kitchen counter, or when you agree to go on a trip, unwillingly, and on the day of departure you sprain your ankle at the train station. It's your mind betraying you through a physical gesture. It's your inner self taking over and making the decisions that your conscious self was unable to make.

I studied psychology, I know the phenomenon. So does he.

"Call me back when you're ready," he says, and hangs up.

We both know what he really means. That I will never call back.

I've lost the man with whom I'd lived for seven years. And I was supposed to share my story with a bunch of stressed out executives.

Never in a million years.

A November evening in Cuneo for a literary festival.

I'm having dinner with a journalist. We'd met for the first time that afternoon. We took an instant liking to each other, instinctively, so much that she asks if we couldn't continue the evening with a drink at a nearby pub. I accept.

Alcohol lubricates our conversation, making it more personal. In a few short hours we've gone from being strangers to confidants, which does happen every so often, for no explicable reason.

At one point she reaches out her right hand for a bottle of water that the waiter has set on the table and suddenly I see it: the vertical scar along the vein on her wrist. She notices my gaze and does not change her expression. She looks at me, with clear, serene eyes.

Yet another confession between us, this time with no need for words.

After that night I will never see her again.

She would die a year later, at a young age, in a war zone.

A risk that she more than others had been ready to take.

I had no previous experience of suicide. By which I mean that I didn't know anyone who had lost a friend, a partner, or a sibling to an act of self-harm. Suicides are something we read about in novels or newspapers, something that happens in broken families or under shocking circumstances. They're not supposed to happen to you.

One reason for the disorientation, the sense of alienation I felt after the death of S., is the singularity of his act. In a tragic way, I myself had become a part of that singular event.

People talked about me in my apartment building, at the agency where I worked, within my circle of friends and acquaintances. I was the unhappy protagonist of a rare event.

And I had no terms of comparison, no models to instruct me.

My suffering felt perversely unique and special.

I have always sought a form of salvation in books.

(How do people save themselves without books?)

This time, however, it's hard; there are few if any texts on survivors, even in scholarly journals. I have to look elsewhere.

But I do find consolation in publications that are embarrassing—when you consider their contents and my intellectual abilities—books that in any other period I would have scorned and made fun of: books by psychics.

I read them the same way some people subscribe to travel magazines, knowing they will never visit the exotic islands pictured in them. (I've heard that most travel-magazine subscribers are people who don't travel; flipping through the pages sublimates the journeys they will never take.)

I don't necessarily believe the things that psychics say in these childish and sensationalistic books, but I hope they're right.

The stories are always a variation on the same theme: The deceased is well, has reached a peaceful place, and wishes to communicate with living family members to reassure them that from his or her location in the afterlife (whatever form it might take), he or she is watching over them, loves them, and is protecting them.

One psychic talks about love after life, telling stories of people who have loved each other through the ages and manage to relive past relationships through hypnotic regression. At any other time, I might have found it asphyxiating to have to repeat the same relationship at another moment in time, in a form of unconscious obsession (then again, at any other time I would never have read a book like this). Now I find it consoling. S. and I have already loved each other and we will love each other again. His suicide is just a bump in the road, a momentary gap in the eternal relationship that binds us and is destined to continue for all time. I find it helpful to think in these terms, to reimagine my situation in the context of a teenager's fantasy fiction. After all, if suburban housewives can read Harlequin romances and fantasize about being carried away by the handsome heir to a small fortune, then why am I not entitled to indulge in transcendental hypotheses that console me and relieve me from the burden that has chained me to the earth for months and months?

I use statistics as an excuse: If there are so many of these books in the bookstores, and so many people believe in them, and the mediums are all saying the same thing, then there must be some truth to it, right?

This is what the books I am reading all tell me, which suits me just fine.

Amy Biancolli, an American journalist, survived the death of her husband, who left her with three children to raise on her own. She examines the practical aspects of post-suicide life in a TEDx Talk that can be seen on YouTube, titled "You're Still Here: Living After Suicide." About halfway through, she mentions a list that she made. A list of reminders that she stuck to her refrigerator door so she would see it every day, several times a day.

The list includes a number of recommendations that we all take for granted but that no longer come to us automatically after a shock. Some of the words on her list are: Live, Be Present, Pray, Laugh, Love.

Biancolli reminds herself that it is her job to continue to live (for her children, for example), to smile whenever possible, to continue to love (opening yourself to love can be scary because it makes you vulnerable, and after the heartbreak of losing someone you love, you never want to feel that way again).

She also mentions the word "learn": Learn to do new things. She chose to learn jazz violin.

To an outside viewer, while these basic actions might seem obvious, there is a logic to them. The recommendation to learn new things is less obvious: The post-suicide period does not seem to be the right time to study or take classes. Who would have the will, the strength, the focus?

Instead her suggestion is a simplified way of describing a much broader and deeper perspective: the need to imagine a future for yourself.

To learn new things means moving forward, continuing to grow, thinking in terms of evolution.

To explore interests unrelated to the person you've lost, and not another shared memory, is the first concrete step toward your next chapter in life, in which new acquaintances will belong to *you* and not to *the two of you*.

The list not only helped her to survive the present, it also made her start thinking about the future again.

(**I thought to** myself: Studying jazz violin is a weird choice. And a second later: What a sensible decision, I understand where she's coming from.)

Start listening to music again.
    Join a gym.
    Try to write (anything).
    Try not to be too much of a downer with your friends.
    Travel to places where you never went together.
    Stay in this apartment for as long as you need.

This is the list I would have written.

(**"Join a gym"** is obviously my version of "study jazz violin.")

Not even a month after S.'s death, the intercom rings early one morning, must be around four o'clock. I wake up with a start. Am I dreaming? The house is immersed in silence. Down on the street all you can hear is the distant sound of the few cars still around at this hour.

A second ring erases my doubts. I get up and go to answer it. "Yes?"

"S. is that you?" asks a boy's voice.

"Who is it?" I ask, but there is no answer. I hear him holding his breath and then the sound of footsteps.

I drop the handset and rush into the bedroom, to the window overlooking the street. I make it just in time to catch a glimpse of a figure in jeans and a T-shirt turning the corner, disappearing from my field of vision.

Who was he?

Not a friend, not a mutual acquaintance, that much is clear. They all know what happened, and they wouldn't be dropping by unannounced at four o'clock in the morning. And they wouldn't run away at the sound of my voice.

He must have been a recent acquaintance of S. A lover. Someone who hasn't heard from him for weeks and doesn't know how to get ahold of him, who calls a number only to find out that it is no longer active, and who, in a moment of desperation, goes to his house looking for him, hoping to find him there asleep.

I remain at the window with the illogical assumption that he will retrace his steps, but the sidewalks are empty, no one is leaving, no one is coming back.

I'm not bothered or upset by the idea that he might have been a lover. Who cares. Who cares about anything.

I just wish that he would come back so that I could explain to him what happened.

I wish I could hug him and cry on his shoulder.

We lost him, I would say through my tears. We have lost him forever. And I would hold him tight, this boy, who shared his body and his scent, this boy, my brother.

Tiziana had a friend, Patrizia, whose name she would mention from time to time. A woman she'd met while on vacation in the mountains, who claimed she had psychic abilities. She could sense things, predict the future.

I didn't hide my skepticism, but Tiziana swore that the woman's powers were real. "She's said things about me that no one knows." As proof of her legitimacy, she added that Patrizia did not make a living from clairvoyance but owned a hair salon, keeping her gift a secret. The only time she took advantage of her talent was the occasional trip to a casino to beat the house (she could predict the winning numbers).

I filed away in my memory the story of the hairdresser and her powers as an amusing tidbit, and had no interest in looking into it further.

I did get the chance to meet her once. She was in Milan for a visit and dropped by the agency to take Tiziana out for lunch. In the office she shook my hand and we introduced ourselves. The only words we exchanged were our names. Tizi grabbed her jacket, and the two of them went out.

When she came back from lunch, Tizi told me that Patrizia could tell that I emanated positive energy, that I was a benevolent presence.

I teased her. "What bullshit. And if she had told you I was a negative presence, what would you have done? Changed offices? Changed jobs?"

We laughed about it and that was the end of the story.

After that I never saw her again.

The morning after S. committed suicide, I phoned Tiziana. I had to ask her to inform the office that I would be absent for a few days. I wanted her to be the one who explained the situation, to tell everyone on my behalf what had happened.

That was perhaps one of the only calls that I made in the first few hours, that I forced myself to make. All the others I delegated.

On the phone I tried to use as few words as possible. One word more and I would have fallen to pieces.

She listened, quietly, and then said something incredible: "Patrizia called me last night. She sensed that something horrific had happened to you."

"She was right," I said, and hung up. I couldn't elaborate any further.

In later years I've often reflected on how extraordinary this circumstance was.

I realize that a few psychics appear in this story, a strange fit for someone like me, who doesn't believe in the paranormal and might not, in fact, believe in anything. But out of all of them, Patrizia's experience is by far the most inexplicable and the most significant. I wonder why, in those early months of anguish and potential openness to the unknowable, I didn't try to see her again. I don't know. At the time, I wasn't lucid enough to make a lot of decisions. In a sense I was drawn toward things that I didn't resist.

Now, at a distance of twenty years, it wouldn't make sense to get to the root of it.

This episode reminds me of the butterfly effect. On a cosmic level something happened: S. stopped beating his wings, and in the thick of night a woman in the Alps felt the earthquake that it had provoked inside of me.

If you wish to believe, believe.

In the late 1990s I published my first novel. It was the story of my adolescence and my first steps into adulthood. The end of the book coincided with the beginning of my living with a man whom I had met and with whom I had fallen in love.

That man was S.

By the time I had finished writing the manuscript and started to send it out for publishers to read, it had been six years since S. and I had first met, and our relationship was on the rocks.

I completed the final version of the text during the summer that the two of us broke up.

S. killed himself in November 1998. The book came out in May 1999.

From the moment the book was published, I found myself dealing simultaneously with my still-raw grief over his loss and a book tour throughout Italy to promote a novel that talked about him. A him that was alive, cheerful, in love, and content. A portrait in ecstatic terms. And I was on tour introducing him.

I've always been passionate about writing. Ever since I was a child, I have preferred to stay home filling up notebooks while my buddies were scraping their knees playing soccer in the playground in front of our building.

Around the age of ten I was already making my own little books—folding sheets of notebook paper in half—complete with a title and a drawing on the cover. A single-copy edition, since I ignored the production and distribution sides of publication. This wasn't a problem: After all, I was writing them for myself, for the pleasure of seeing these make-believe volumes with my name on the cover. They were stories of pirates, submarines, dragons and princesses, explorers. Nothing about them was original; they were copied from stories the teacher used to read in school. Half the time I didn't even finish them: I would focus on the title, the cover, write a few pages, and then stop for dinner; the next day I would already be planning another story, fascinated more by the production side than by the contents. I was practicing writing long before I had anything to say.

For years I kept my vocation for writing under the radar, as if it were a personal habit. I didn't admit to myself that I wanted to take it seriously until I was in college, when for the first time I started writing texts with an eye to circulating them. Mostly short stories.

And a whole novel, which I eventually tossed out without showing it to anyone because I realized it was just an experiment, my own personal workout to get ready for a bigger project. I was flexing my muscles to see if I was strong enough.

I was in no hurry. I gave myself time.

By nature I'm frantic and impulsive, and I don't know why it is that in the field of writing I managed to be something I was incapable of being in other endeavors: patient.

I thought about writing all the time. I tried to imagine what it would be like to publish my own book, with a real publisher, and present it at bookstores where I'd meet my readers.

But when that moment arrived, the timing couldn't have been worse.

The first presentation, my first ever, took place in a movie theater during a film retrospective. I remember the excitement and the anxiety at finding myself standing in front of a full house. Being there was both exciting and excruciating. It put my strength to the test. I kept my gaze fixed on the back row, on distant faces, which is to say, on no one. I was happy to be there and at the same time I felt guilty for being happy. I smiled and answered, almost in a trance, the questions of the woman who introduced me, another writer. I felt as if I were someone else, my heart was beating a mile a minute, the blood was racing through my veins, the lights, the people, the buzz in the house, the applause, as if the experience as a whole had crashed into me and I had to bear the impact. This is too much, a voice inside me said, way too much.

The conversation took place during the interval between films at the festival, fifteen minutes: I could not have managed anything longer.

Some friends had come to support me and were sitting in the front row. Afterward one of them complained, "You never looked in our direction, not even once."

Because I was not there, I wanted to tell him. I don't know who that mannequin was impersonating me.

Smile. Wave. Applause.

It's amazing how functional you can become.

Better yet: You split in two.

You learn to have two faces, one for the outside world and one that is private.

You learn to take ownership of this duality. To recognize that you are entitled to it.

Grief is an acting class.

You learn to pretend with everyone. You go out, talk, smile, mingle with others, reassure, assure people that you're coping, that you're hanging in there.

On the inside a hellfire is burning and hollowing you out.

On the outside you act normal.

At first it's difficult, you don't fool anyone. They know what happened to you, and they expect you to grieve.

Over time you become more credible, show that you've supposedly gotten better. They almost always fall for it. They want to fall for it.

From that point on you rely on improvisation, a button you manage to push every time, in public.

Not only do you become an actor; you become a very good one.

You deserve an Academy Award for Best Actor and no one knows except you.

To lose someone so suddenly throws your life into upheaval: Nothing has prepared you for such a shock. Illness or old age places us gradually in the frame of mind to accept the inevitable, but a tragic death (an accident, a shooting, cardiac arrest) crashes into our everyday life with the intensity of an earthquake, leaving us devastated.

We have to come to terms with a fundamental absence that was unexpected; it seems impossible to us that anything could happen so abruptly and irrevocably, and we aren't able to make sense of it.

But when someone performs such a brutal act voluntarily, everything becomes complicated, our feelings turn in on themselves and get tangled up inextricably: Anger spills over into love, regret is accompanied by resentment, and feelings of guilt conflict with the feeling you've been deceived.

You need answers. You need order. A context in which things can be right or wrong and not so perversely indistinguishable.

People who are mourning a suicide victim are filled with contradictions. Their grief is never as pure as grief over a simple loss. Their pain is dirty, murky. A labyrinth.

As for me, already wallowing in this well of incongruities, I added another, the most spectacular of them all: an audience.

The book presentation was part of my therapy, a contorted mechanism for processing mourning that involved talking about him repeatedly while hiding the real issue from everyone.

The first meetings with the public were difficult. Questions about S. were always popping up: Are you still together? What does he think about the book? Is he here tonight? There would be the occasional wise ass: "Will you introduce me to him?" And the room would burst into laughter. I would laugh, too. "No, he's not here," I'd reply, suppressing the word that should have fallen at the end of the sentence, the "anymore" that would have made his absence permanent.

This constant evocation of S. inured me to his absence.

In my own way I had told the truth. I had revealed it immediately, on the first page of the book.

The dedication that appears at the beginning of the novel reads: "To S., wherever you may be, this book is for you."

I thought it was so clear, so explicit: To write "wherever you may be" made it obvious that he was no longer here among us.

I was convinced I had said too much, and thought that everyone would guess.

But no one even noticed.

On that first book tour, I learned many things, one in particular: that when you write about yourself you draw boundaries, you choose what to tell and what not to tell, who to include and who to leave out of the story. These are boundaries that you've thought about and that meet certain criteria. For you. Not for the readers; they want to know more, to know everything. As if you'd given them a taste and now they want the whole meal.

They asked me about my parents, my sister, my hometown. They wanted all the things I'd decided to omit, intimate details, slices of the past, present, and future.

I realized that I had to set limits on their curiosity and their questions. That I had to defend myself.

It was a matter of both artistic principle and personal need.

I needed to defend all the characters in the book, but the incident concerning S. made it critical.

I did learn to share a few things. For example, that S. had read and liked the book (he'd seen an advance draft of it, typewritten). That I was not willing to talk about my love life, only about the contents of the novel. The novel concerned the recent past: My present situation was irrelevant.

I had to defend myself and to defend the contents of the book, which told a story of acceptance and joy. To speak of what would happen years later, of that shocking and devastating event, would have distorted the meaning.

S. and I had tastes in music that could not have been further apart, so we never looked for common ground, knowing it would be a waste of time. Nor did we try to convert each other. (What's the point of being with someone different if you try to make them just like you?)

He enjoyed listening to Italian singer-songwriters, the latest dance hits, and an occasional singer from the 1960s. An absurd combination (like the musical tastes of each and every one of us).

Me, I preferred English new wave, some Italian indies, Björk. An equally absurd combination (like the musical tastes of each and every one of us).

We created our own private listening spaces. Me in the office (Tiziana and I often worked with the door closed and a portable radio with the volume on low); he in the car or when he was driving the van.

We would also listen to music at home every now and then, taking turns: I would let him listen to one CD, then I would take over.

A balancing game.

In the last months of his life, S. listened to only one album, over and over. He was obsessed with a ten- or twelve-year-old record, the debut album of an Italian singer-songwriter, the classic case of a one-hit wonder. But S. was not interested in that famous single; he was obsessed with another song, a minor track that was an ode to the father figure, the love song of a son for a departed parent.

I didn't find the song particularly moving. Even the lyrics were weak, but for S. they clearly had a special meaning.

When someone disappears so abruptly and irrevocably, you can't help but think back to the days preceding their death in search of a telltale sign.

His obsession with this song was yet another clue that had somehow escaped my grasp.

In the notebook of letters he left me, which I no longer had the courage to reread, there is one passage etched in my memory:

> When I left home I said I was going to my
>   mother's. I lied.
> I'm going to my father's.

S. had never met his father, who died two months before he was born.
As he was planning his suicide, he prepared himself symbolically to meet him.

S. loved driving, and with him I discovered that I liked being driven. I didn't have to worry about a thing, he knew where to go, how to get there, and how long it would take. All I had to do was occupy the seat next to him and allow myself to be driven.

I've always experienced driving as a necessity, never a pleasure. If I have to travel, I'll use public transportation, take the train. Seeing someone who really enjoyed driving was a revelation (the constant amazement at learning that other people are not like us, which is so fascinating the first time you realize it).

In the early days he would pick me up in his car, then we would drive around at night. When he brought me back, sometimes late, very late, it would take him a good half hour to drive to his own place: He didn't seem to mind in the least.

Many of our deepest conversations took place inside the car, as if traveling gave us permission to question each other; I would ask him something, then he would ask me. This is how we got to know each other, on the road.

I also learned some of his worst shortcomings, like his awful habit of throwing cans out the window when they were empty, which I put a stop to immediately.

It was during one of those short but endless journeys on the outskirts of our lives that he told me a funny episode from his childhood.

His mother was a widow with four children. He was the youngest. She worked in a factory to support them, and depended on her neighbors' support to care for the children when she was out. S. was the unruliest of the four (of course). He was a pain in the neck: He couldn't sit still and would scrape his knees playing in the courtyard, or get scratched up from falling off his bike along the streets of the town. The neighbors had their hands full keeping up with him. And sometimes they had commitments of their own and could not help out. On days like that the poor woman had to find some way to keep S. at home and prevent him from causing a ruckus. So she came up with an unusual method: In the morning, before leaving for the factory, she would dress him in his sister's clothes. S. wouldn't have the guts to be seen by other children in that ridiculous getup. Homespun genius; the trick worked. S. stayed within the four walls and dedicated himself to quieter games. Until he managed to find a way to turn the tables. One day, in defiance of fate, he joined his friends wearing that absurd attire. Before anyone could make fun of him, he announced, "Let's play carnival! I've already got my costume!" His little friends greeted the idea with enthusiasm and ran home to look for accessories they could use to dress up. So he managed to beat his mother at her own game!

He had a satisfied smirk on his face when he told me the story. I could almost picture him, little S. with a sly, victorious grin on his face.

Maybe this was the quality that won me over from the start: the flashes of pure innocence that peeked through his tough-guy exterior.

Doctors and psychologists didn't used to recommend psychopharmaceuticals to alleviate mental disturbances back then. I imagine that the people who did ask for them were generally refused. I didn't ask for anything.

Every now and then I would stumble across a newspaper article or television program about addiction to antianxiety pills and antidepressants, and on the gravity of a phenomenon that was spreading like the plague. Almost every American movie and TV show would feature a woman scarred by her abuse of pills, although she had no particular reason to take them.

Bored housewives sought the salvation that I disdained.

Every now and then a friend, seeing me looking haggard, would suggest, "Why don't you get a prescription for something to feel better? Just till you make it through this period."

I would shake my head.

I didn't want to feel better. I mean, of course, I hoped the grief would ease up and let me breathe, and that the sheer weight of it would diminish with time. But deep inside I knew that I had to go through this suffering in order to come out of it, rather than work my way around it.

The idea that a pill could give me back my smile, my joy, seemed grotesque to me in that moment. A magic potion that could turn me into a serene man, in my eyes, was monstrous.

I already felt like enough of a monster for not having saved him. That should be enough.

"The pain of my loss was all that was left of him. It tore me apart, but I had no wish to dull the agony with painkillers. It was confirmation that he had lived, that he had been my husband. I did not want that to be gone as well."

—LITT WOON LONG,
*THE WAY THROUGH THE WOODS:
ON MUSHROOMS AND MOURNING*

A few months after the death of S., I get a phone call. "Hi, this is Cristina."

I recognize her voice immediately, although it's been ages since we last got together.

We met when we were both eighteen or so. She lived in a town near mine and became a part of our group thanks to a mutual friend's intercession. She was the first Buddhist I had ever met (in the years to come I would meet others, but at the time she was the only one) and so, partly to distinguish her from the other Cristina in our group, we called her "Cristina the Buddhist." For us her religion became her last name.

We saw each other frequently for several years, and then, for no particular reason except the different directions in which our lives went, we lost touch. She got engaged to a man from her congregation, then they moved in together in an apartment in the Brianza area since they had both found jobs there and it was close to their main temple. Gradually the two of us drifted apart.

Hearing her voice again plunged me into the past. "Cristina," I say. "It's been so long!"

She doesn't waste time with small talk, that's not why she's called.

"I wanted to tell you that Federico died last night. He felt sick in the bathroom. I called the ambulance but there was nothing they could do. A brain aneurysm."

I fell silent, caught completely off guard (by her phone call, by this voyage in time, by the dramatic news).

"The funeral service will be Saturday afternoon at the temple, if you'd like to come."

I am surprised but not incredulous. I understand why she called me despite the years of oblivion. When death breaks into your daily life from one moment to the next, you're so bewildered that you find yourself operating by instinct, making decisions whose meaning may not be entirely clear to you, but whose urgency is all that matters. Like calling every number in your datebook to share your grief with as many people as possible.

I don't tell her, but I understand her. Oh, do I ever. "Of course, I'll be there on Saturday," I promise.

I'd never been to a Buddhist funeral before, and I didn't even know if they called them funerals.

The ceremony takes place in a room of the temple, and the atmosphere is palpably much more serene and calm than any Catholic funeral. For Buddhists, death is a positive concept: We are celebrating his passing, not mourning his earthly demise.

Friends at the microphone tell anecdotes about Federico and remember his characteristics. The people in attendance nod and sometimes smile.

I see Cristina from a distance. She is surrounded by family members and girlfriends. She seems at peace, although I imagine she has a bottomless pit inside. I ignore the possibility that something extraordinary is cradled in her serenity.

When the testimonies conclude, she gets up and goes to the piano (there was a piano in the room, which I hadn't noticed before). She sits down, lifts the cover to the keyboard, and starts to play the sweet melody of a famous song. Only when she begins to sing do I recognize it: Gershwin's "The Man I Love."

I'm instantly moved to tears.

I didn't know that Cristina could play the piano or sing. Maybe these were talents that she kept hidden from us, or maybe they came to her later.

She sings the whole song, voice never cracking, without giving in to emotion.

I listen to her and can't help but think that she's extraordinary.

What a splendid gesture, to dedicate a piece like that to your deceased man. And to do so at his funeral ceremony, with a smile, is stoic.

At the funeral of S., I would not have been able to say a single word in public, much less give a performance.

When I hug her at the end of the ceremony, half an hour later, she says nothing, and neither do I. The closeness of our bodies is the only message that we exchange spontaneously. But deep inside I keep thinking: To me you are a hero.

I'm writing this book because I wish that back then I could have read a book like this, about the grief of those left behind.

But writing it also means asking myself new questions, seeking new lines of inquiry. I remember how isolated and lonely I felt back then, and realize that if I had to face a similar experience today, things would be very different: All you have to do is go online to find hundreds of Web sites in a wide variety of fields. This also makes me wonder if it would make any sense to search for the types of comfort I longed for then, although I no longer have a pressing need.

The one avenue where it might make sense to conduct new research is the thing I needed most back then: to share my feelings with other people who had experienced the same trauma, who would understand the exact meaning of this unique form of agony.

A self-help group specifically for relatives of suicide victims.

Does one exist?

Despite the profusion of digital resources online, I wasn't able to find anything right away. I send a bunch of emails, make phone calls, and am referred to one contact person after another.

I find various support groups for bereaved relatives, but none of them are designed specifically for family members of suicide victims. I'm given the name of the coordinator of one such group, in Emilia, who is himself the relative of a suicide victim. I manage to get his cell-phone number. His name is Nicola. I phone him, tell him who I am and about the book I am writing, and ask him if he'd be willing to meet to talk to me about his experience. He is rather cold and reticent, at least on the phone, but he agrees, and we decide to meet toward the end of the month.

Meanwhile my search for specific groups continues until I find one.

There is only one, apparently. In Padua.

The sessions take place once a week.

I call the number of the office and ask if I can attend at least a few sessions. The kind manager explains that she has to submit my question to the group and that she'll let me know. A few days later she calls back to inform me that only some of the participants are willing to meet with me. We try to set a date.

And then the unimaginable happens. COVID-19 breaks out in Italy, and a lockdown, a total closure, is announced.

A terrifying, urgent reality interrupts my belated attempt to write about grief.

A message from the cosmos: Who cares about your old trauma? We have more urgent problems to deal with today.

The present seeks to deprive me of meaning.

THE NATURAL FACILITATOR

In the early days of the lockdown I can't force myself to do anything, let alone write. I make it through the first phase in an almost catatonic state, as did many, I would later find out.

But then comes the need to snap out of it, to react.

When isolation is prolonged and the weeks start to go by with no indication as to when and how we will be able to start traveling again, to meet in person, I realize that certain experiences, like live participation in a group, will be postponed for months. In some cases, however, I might be able to adapt to the circumstances.

I was supposed to meet with Nicola, from the self-help group in Emilia. I decide to contact him again and propose that we do a video chat. He schedules an appointment for five o'clock the next day.

He answers my call from the living room of his house. He's ironing. I'm amused by our circumstances (talking about death while performing domestic duties: a combination of thanatology and home economics).

Nicola is a bachelor in his mid-thirties and is going through isolation alone, as his ironing would seem to indicate.

The first question I ask him is what it means to be a facilitator and why he decided to become one.

He explains that he is a "natural facilitator," by which he does not mean that it comes to him spontaneously; it is a technical term. Facilitators are usually professionals, and it is their job to coordinate the activities of the self-help group. A natural facilitator, on the other hand, is a member of the group who becomes its coordinator: not a psychologist, educator, or therapist, but rather a person who has addressed the trauma of grief through a collective reflection and is now placing his experience at the service of others.

In the first few minutes of our conversation, while he is sharing this information with me, Nicola keeps on ironing, and then gradually leaves the iron on the ironing board and focuses all his attention on me.

I ask him whether he has noticed any differences between the grieving of the relatives of a suicide victim and that of family members whose loved one died of another cause. He answers that, in one way or another, everyone feels remorse and guilt about the person who has passed away, but for survivors the feeling is much more intense: "With an illness or an accident, there isn't much you can do. With a suicide, on the other hand, at the end of the day you always feel that if you had said certain things, gone to see him that day, paid closer attention to his words, you could have done something. You could have saved him."

During our first phone call, Nicola indicated some reservations. From the outset he said that he would not tell me his story, and he was not interested in sharing it. He was so guarded that you could tell his feelings were still very raw.

During our video call, by contrast, the longer we spoke, the more he lowered his resistance. First he tells me he has lost "two important family members," in a very general way, without providing further clues. Then, unconsciously or spontaneously, he starts to reveal the details. I learn that he lost his mother about fifteen years ago and his older brother, to suicide, four years ago. It is about this loss that he is most reticent. "Even today I can't talk about it with others. With my colleagues at work, for instance. If anyone asks me, I say it was an accident, so I avoid the conversation. They wouldn't understand anyway. There's always prejudice toward suicides, as if the person brought it on himself or deserved it. People don't know what might be behind it," he tells me.

At first, he avoids using the term "suicide," adopting an odd circumlocution instead: "My brother made another life choice." A minute later he adds, "I know I'm playing with words, but that's what I still prefer to call it."

I understand. A survivor needs to use the language that he considers appropriate. He also has to find a way to tell this story to himself.

What stood out for me in his account was the fact that his brother, although he lived in another city with his wife and children, chose to return to his parents' home to commit the act.

He tells me that, in the days that followed, everyone was asking the same question: "Why did he do it?"

But the question his father asked was: "Why did he do it *here*?"

I ask Nicola if he was able to find an answer. He says that he was, believing that the main reason for his brother's choice was pragmatic: "I think he wanted to protect his children from seeing."

We go back to talking about the group. I want to understand, based on his experience, what he considered the most important form of support it provided.

"First and foremost, empathy; it makes you feel that you are not the only person suffering in this way," he replies without hesitation.

He is keen to point out, however, that the people who attend the group do not just take something away, they also give something back. That there is a mutual exchange.

"The first few times I attended meetings, I thought they were a waste of time, that I had nothing in common with the others. I used to attend without speaking, and all I did was listen. I realized then that to simply listen was also important. It occurred to me because I felt the need to go back. And once I did, I never left again."

He concludes with a statement that touches me deeply. "There are some people whose grief is so stubborn that they don't realize they have something to give so they end up leaving after a couple of sessions. Not everyone is ready."

The stubbornness of their grief.

Their inability to understand that grief is something you can share, or rather, that you can give to others.

I wonder about my own stubbornness in the past two decades.

I keep thinking of that detail of the brother returning to his father's house to take his own life, and of the father's (unanswered) question: Why here?

Nicola is right when he says that he wanted to spare his children from witnessing the trauma. His choice of location was premeditated.

The brother chose his childhood home, where he had already lost his mother, where there was already a familiarity, an acquaintance with grief. Where there was someone who could accept him.

S. chose to kill himself in our home because it allowed him to spare his mother. He knew that I would take care of things, after which his sister and brothers would find a way to protect the elderly woman (and they did). A (minimal) containment of the consequences.

His choice of location can be seen in two ways: either he wanted to inflict it on me, or he was relying on me, for the sake of the love that had bound us together for years.

I was his last act of trust at a moment when he had lost trust in everything else.

I had to lean toward the second option. I had no choice. I wouldn't have survived the first.

When Nicola says that he doesn't speak about his brother's suicide with others, with colleagues, since they wouldn't understand, he makes me reflect on myself: Why don't I speak about S.'s, either? Why is it that the colleagues, the friends whom I've met in recent years, are unaware of this story?

Am I ashamed? I wonder.

No, I don't feel at all embarrassed by the subject. I'm not afraid of being judged, nor do I care what they might think of S. (besides, they never met him).

What is it then? What should I call this feeling?

Reticence? Discretion?

"The most important thing is that I don't want to be ashamed of my existence. I don't want to lie about it. I didn't write the book to be hurtful to people, but the truth can be hurtful."
—A. M. HOMES, *WHY WE WRITE ABOUT OURSELVES*

Why did it take me so long to tell this story? I don't have an answer and I have a multitude of answers.

What I would say is that in order to begin, you have to tell yourself what happened, and there is no single set of words to do so. It is a story that changes over time, evolving, finding new terminology and new forms, growing. It ages with you.

In the beginning you have to tell it to yourself, the first thing you do the moment you open your eyes in the morning. This is your reality, now go and remember what happened to you.

It's an inverted REM cycle, in which waking up is the nightmare.

You'll need months just to learn to live with it.

When you're busy surviving, you don't worry too much about how to convey this story to the outside world. You leave to others the job of understanding. It's a narrative made up of omissions; the withheld tears, the silences, are the protagonists to whom you must turn to figure out the rest of the story.

For a period you feel like you'll never recover. (They constantly tell you, "You'll see. Things will get better," but what the fuck do they know? You don't believe anyone.)

And when slowly, very slowly, things do start to get better, when you catch a glimmer of a future, you grab hold of it. Then the tragedy (which still leaves a scar on the rest of your life) turns into something to be managed, like a piece of furniture that you keep moving around the room and at times manage to place in a spot where you can't see it. You know full well that it's always present—over there, right next to you, behind you—but in the meantime, you can also look out the window, look ahead.

With time that bulky piece of furniture becomes more manageable, shrinking to a size that is easier to move, and you become proficient at dealing with it. (Am I saying it's a monstrosity? You become fond of it. In the sense that you learn to think of it with a dose of benevolence, of affection.) You see it as one of many elements in the room, no longer the main one.

It is a process that takes years.

As time passed, I came to realize that (at least in my case) not only does the narrative vary; so does your willingness to tell it. I've become reticent. I only tell some people, and only in certain circumstances.

When you start to feel better, you commit to maintaining that serenity. You work at it. You know how fragile you can be and that you're skating on thin ice. You have to protect yourself. One way is to decide not to tell the story so often, not to reopen the wound.

You feel sorry for yourself.

But in me two souls coexist: the person and the writer.

The person addresses things in one way, the writer in another.

The writer is curious, obsessive. He fixates on details, and takes note of everything. As he faces the abyss, he wants to peer inside of it rather than save himself. He is drawn to horror. He feels like both guinea pig and eyewitness.

He places the story in a conceptual safe-deposit box, shapes it, reworks it. He returns to it obsessively. He preserves it.

If there's one thing I've learned about myself, with regard to writing, it's that I need time. I have to place an emotional distance between myself and events. When I write a story, I have to leave it locked in a drawer for a while before I go back to reread it and figure out whether it really does have a meaning, a value. When I write about myself, about my experiences, I have to wait for months, for years, before I can approach the story with the proper detachment, with the necessary objectivity.

It was inevitable that I would recount my portable hell, the one I have been carrying on my back since then, but finding the right emotional distance turned out to be more complicated than expected.

So I do not have one answer, I have multitudes.

This book has been easier to write than to conceive. It works and makes sense as long as I'm here in this room re-creating grief on a keyboard. And afterward? How am I supposed to handle a confession like this?

The first time I spoke with my agent about this project, she asked: Are you ready?

As if to say: Are you ready to deliver it to the outside world, to speak about it in public, to answer the questions that will come, to deal with people's reactions, to attend events, presentations, and interviews, to see this work as a book, with everything that entails?

My answer was and is: I don't know. I don't know if I'm ready. Even now, on the brink of the irrevocable, I don't know.

I'm not ashamed to talk about it, but I am aware of the gravity of the thing I am placing in the hands of my listeners.

It is the opposite of a gift: Why inflict such punishment on anyone?

Each of us has lights, each has shadows.

Mine is not just a shadow: It's an eclipse that can cast everything into darkness.

"What seemed most outlandish in our autobiography is what really happened."
—STEVE ABBOTT, "ELEGY"

There is something else I do during the lockdown, in this absurd limbo we are living through, on a planet paralyzed by fear, a muffled silence outside the window even in a metropolis like Milan. In the midst of the isolation, I respond to the signals I have been intercepting for some time now.

I come to find out that a writer I know, only slightly (we met once at a book fair), is also a survivor. His wife took her life a few months ago.

To my knowledge, he has not spoken about it publicly, but every now and then, on social media, he indulges in brief, lacerating confessions.

Once he wrote:

> I often cry while I'm driving the car, with this empty seat next to me.
> Sometimes I sing along with the radio or talk to myself, while other times I let out a cry filled with anger or life or both.
> But the car, like life, continues on, regardless.

Another:

When you experience terrible grief, people tell you: you have to move on. But the truth is, you have to go through it.

His posts are like a message in a bottle sent to whoever might find it, and today I am one of those people.

The time has come to hear from him, so I send an email.

I don't know if my request might seem inopportune, whether it is intruding rudely into a moment of grief that is still warm, made all the more alienating by the ongoing state of emergency.

I try to let him know that he doesn't have to answer, that a simple no would be acceptable.

But the next day he writes me an email, long and beautiful, part confession, part storytelling, part sharing.

A letter that acknowledges me as a fellow griever.

After reading it, I have a burning desire to jump in the car and drive, join him in his city by the sea, meet him that same day and talk late into the night. I wish we could exhaust our words, confide in each other every nuance of despair, show each other every chink in our armor. But we can't. There's a government decree, checkpoints on the roads, and a deadly virus lurking insidiously. We are forced into immobility.

So I reread his email. Two, three, five times. And his words already seem to contain anything that he might have to say to me in person.

On his incessant inner conflict:

> There's no need to tell you how I'm struggling with enormous feelings of guilt.
> What did I not understand, what did I do wrong, what could I and should I have done, would she have been better off without me, how could I have failed so badly, I who was supposed to protect her, she who considered me a blessing, the best thing in her life.
> But if that's true, then why was I not enough?

On the unique sentiment felt by those left behind:

As much as people might try to understand how I feel, I am really the only one who has to carry this enormous burden, and it's hard to share, and sometimes, if only to avoid contaminating others, you don't talk about it, or people are afraid to ask so they don't ask you anything and you suffer because you think: How is it possible that they don't understand the awful moment I'm going through?

For months I identified with my grief, I felt as if the people I knew, even without saying so, saw me as only "poor guy, the one whose wife took her own life," because in effect that is how I feel, my loss still overwhelms everything, casting it in the shadows, taking away even my memories of happier times.

On the hope that one day he will be able to overcome this and find something positive, even in this situation:

I hope time will allow me to look at this part of life with less horror and pain, and thereby regain love and kindness and forgiveness for both me and her.
Who knows.

His words are mine. They are the things we all say to ourselves when we've been randomly chosen for this fate.

The script we improvise for anyone who will listen. The homily of our private ordeal.

Brothers and sisters, we are gathered here.

In my Web searches, the name Maurizio Pompili, a professor of psychiatry at the University of Rome "La Sapienza," starts to pop up regularly. My writer friend also mentioned him, praising his dedication.

Pompili is the head of the Suicide Prevention Center at the Sant'Andrea University Hospital in Rome, the only such facility in Italy. He has devoted several books and a long list of scholarly articles to the subject of suicide. I am eager to meet him, but even after the lockdown ends, it seems to be almost impossible.

I stay in touch with his assistant, Denise, through whom I keep setting up appointments, all of which are ultimately canceled because of the professor's busy schedule.

After a few months of trying, I give up.

But then there is an unexpected turn of events. Denise writes to say that Pompili is holding an online conference on the subject of suicide: Would I be interested in participating as a guest speaker?

This would be the first time I would be telling my story publicly, although through the mediation of a computer.

Would I be interested in participating?
   I don't know whether I am, but I answer yes.

Having come this far, in the middle of writing these pages, what sense would it make to say no?

S. did not have the habit of writing, but he left messages for everyone. And as I said, he left dozens for me.

He bid farewell to life while writing.

I have learned over the years that there are various scholarly studies of the goodbye notes left by suicides. In general they are sociological analyses looking into the most common motives behind the deed.

The notes can contain accusations and complaints, confessions, requests for forgiveness, justifications to family members, declarations of innocence for crimes they were unjustly accused of, practical instructions, and last wishes.

I wonder if there are any literary analyses of these texts: the style, the language, the recurring words. How does a person write their last message to family members, a message that will also be the last trace they bequeath to the world?

A study of the poetics of farewells.

(**I come to** learn that there are also cases—but rarely—of ironic farewells.

The French writer-director Romain Gary, who took his life with a gun while in bed, prepared every detail of the mise-en-scène: He wore a red dressing gown, so that it would blend in with the color of the blood and soften the visual impact; he covered the pillow with a towel to muffle the sound; and he left a note on the bedside table that said, "Never before have I expressed myself so clearly."

In the days before taking the extreme act, Cesare Pavese jotted down various reflections on the subject. Among them a poetic definition stands out: "Suicides are timid murderers." Timid because the murderer turns against himself, not against others. But in the note that he leaves on the bedside table of the hotel room, written before ingesting twelve sachets of a soporific, the last sentence, his final farewell to the world, is a good-natured rebuke: "Try not to gossip too much."

The author of the celebrated novel *Trout Fishing in America*, Richard Brautigan, shot himself in his California home, where he had lived in almost total seclusion. Imagining that his body would not be found for a few weeks, he is rumored to have left a note saying, "Messy, isn't it?")

At the virtual conference organized by Professor Pompili, I told my personal story in front of a few hundred strangers online. It was the first time I had done so publicly, but the remote format meant that I was speaking to the tiny camera of my laptop from my room. I was actually speaking to myself. Like a dress rehearsal in case there would be a live performance in the future.

At the end of my talk, several people wrote comments in the chat room, using words like "courage" and "honesty." It went well, I think.

The professor himself called later to thank me. And he promised that we would meet again.

THE SOLITARY LUMINARY

It's mid-July and Rome is broiling hot. This would be a perfect day to go to the beach rather than to conduct an interview at a hospital, but after almost two years of trying, I'll be meeting today with Dr. Maurizio Pompili, who has finally agreed to see me.

When I finally reach the Sant'Andrea University Hospital, where the Suicide Prevention Center headed by Pompili is located, I stop in the lobby for a few minutes so I can get used to the air-conditioning. And maybe also to prepare myself mentally for what awaits me.

To get to the offices of the center, I have to walk through corridors, take an elevator, go down two sublevels, and follow a series of signs. To be on the safe side, I also reread the instructions that the doctor's assistant sent me. When I get there, after taking two different buses and winding my way through the labyrinth of the hospital, I feel as if I've reached the top level of a video game.

You'd think that a person who dedicates his life to studying suicide might have been motivated by direct, personal experience. Although many people might think so, this is not the case with Dr. Pompili. As a student he became interested in the subject through a course that he took, but his choice was dictated in the end by empathy.

Which is the first thing that he tells me. He is a short, slender man with sharp features framed by a goatee and a pair of thin-rimmed glasses. He looks me straight in the eye as he speaks, from the opposite side of the desk.

"I realized that my life story, with all the pain and emotional upheaval I've suffered, had something in common, in a way, with people contemplating suicide. I've experienced that same type of mental distress, so I was able to approach these patients and maybe help them."

I was surprised by how openly he spoke with me. When I asked what made him choose this field, I had expected a more formal answer rather than a personal account. Perhaps a measure of restraint, of reserve, seems senseless to a man so accustomed to dealing with intense pain every day.

"Compassion is not enough, of course, much more is needed—medication, psychotherapy, scientific expertise—but I believe that the human component can make a difference."

Indeed.

I ask him why there is so little talk of suicide today, even in medical and scientific journals. He explains that the situation is slowly changing, even in the way the issue is studied.

"Suicide has always been seen as a symptom of a mental disorder, while in reality it is a much more complex phenomenon. The standard thinking used to be that people who wish to attempt suicide are depressed, and therefore should be treated with an antidepressant. But that's not entirely true. Many depressed people do not think about death; the ones who do are under constant mental distress, a sense of failure, of anguish, sometimes physical pain, and an endless inner dialogue...to them suicide looks like the best way to escape from that state. Rather than a desire to get closer to death, it is an extreme attempt to be free of a psychological pain that has become unbearable. If their pain could be alleviated or eliminated, they would regain the will to live. Today we try to approach the problem from this perspective."

Although I have wanted this meeting for a long time, I don't have any specific questions prepared. I have nothing on me, not even a piece of paper with scribbled notes. I know I have far too many questions, but I spontaneously ask him something personal, as he did with me. I tell him that when I was dealing with the loss of S., I had looked for some form of support, but found nothing, and in doing my research for this book, I still find very little. I get the impression that in Italy the only centers that exist were established by people for whom this drama is written on their skin. That these centers are, in effect, individual initiatives.

He agrees, telling me that when he started working in the field, in 2005, there was really little or nothing in the way of support. What they have managed to achieve in the past twenty years was accomplished with great difficulty and almost no resources other than personal contributions.

During my research in the past few months, I have come to realize that the work Pompili is doing is so unique that it has made him, despite his wishes, perhaps, the main reference point for any initiative of this type. People who want to establish aid groups or associations end up turning to him. Not least because they can find no one else. Thanks to his support, there are now a number of associations scattered throughout Italy, from Calabria to Puglia to Piedmont. Groups that have maybe a dozen members, if they have any at all.

On his office wall is a map of Italy dotted with colored pushpins marking each town that has a group. Groups for parents who have lost a teenage daughter and are now visiting schools to talk about prevention, or for children with a parent who has taken his or her own life, and organize awareness days. But why is it that they depend solely on volunteer personnel and receive no major financial support from, say, the government?

"There is still very little investment wherever you go, not only in Italy. Partly due to a kind of collective repression, partly because until recently there has never been a reflection on how to prevent suicide. For centuries it has been described, reported, and condemned, but never actively prevented."

I acknowledge that prevention is critical, but there is still another issue: assistance to the victims' families, those who are left behind. Pompili's thoughts on this subject are more sobering.

"It's already difficult to have targeted services for suicide prevention. It will be a long time before we can have them for *survivors*. In fact, right now we don't even have proper protocols on how to help them."

The enormous need of survivors for advice and consolation has been disregarded. Which is why, he tells me, some people travel from far away, taking planes, trains, booking hotels, just to visit the center. He is always amazed by their efforts. "All we can do is listen to them. We wish we could offer so much more."

This might surprise Pompili and his collaborators, but not me. If this resource had existed decades ago, I have no doubt that I, too, would have traveled across Italy to get there. After all, if I'm here today, it's not just to ask questions but to speak with someone who can understand me, even if I am twenty years late.

There is so little consolation available to survivors that simply being listened to by a professional can be a huge help. He is well aware of this. "For many people it is already a form of catharsis to be able to confide in someone who is open to their story and has the diagnostic tools to understand it. We can answer questions they couldn't have even asked at other places. By helping them to understand how a suicidal person acts and thinks, we can dispel their doubts and provide some support."

So then why is there only one such institution, the one here, in all of Italy?

"Because it depends on individual initiative," he admits.

In other words, this center exists only because of him, a man who had the willpower to establish the center and the tenacity to keep it going. There are not many psychiatrists who are willing to take on all the responsibilities connected to having a patient who is a suicide risk. "It's a situation that creates considerable anxiety that not everyone knows how to handle," he tells me. There is also a lack of training, unfortunately. "We have a specialized department because I am here. My students study the issue, but in other medical schools it is rarely if ever mentioned."

I look around the room. We are in the basement of the hospital. The professor's office is a windowless space that requires artificial lighting even in the middle of summer. I attempt a joke: Your location itself is a form of repression.

Pompili laughs for the first time since the start of our conversation. "Ah, no. This is the fate of the whole field of psychiatry, not just those of us who deal with suicide. They always put us in the dungeon! Let me show you something."

He gets up and walks to a series of black-and-white photos on the wall next to his desk. "These men are Edwin Shneidman, Norman Farberow, and Robert Litman, great American psychiatrists, the fathers of the modern field of suicidology. They started the first suicide prevention center in the world in Los Angeles in the 1950s. And they, too, were in the *basement* of a hospital."

It starts from the bottom, then. And although the road may be uphill, one man has fortunately decided to travel it.

The crate of water bottles.

The most heartbreaking detail in my memory, which I've never told anyone, and have always kept to myself.

There was a crate of water bottles next to the door, on the right. Six bottles wrapped in plastic.

S. hung the rope above it.

At the moment of the yank, of the spasms, he could have extended a foot, placed it on the crate, and he would have been safe.

There it was, inches away.

He did not want to save himself. Not even at the last second. Not even when he could have.

A few months have gone by since the death of S, and at a party I meet a guy from Bologna. A mutual friend introduces us, and I stop to chat with him, since he hardly knows anyone here.

I chat with him but I do not see him.

Ever since the tragedy, I no longer relate to other men in terms of attraction or interest. It's the last thing on my mind. I forget faces, names. They pass through me without a trace. The possibility of meeting new people, forging a relationship, seems about as likely to me as embarking on a trip to the moon: pure science fiction.

The man from Bologna is charming and I enjoy chatting with him. At least it passes the time and helps me to avoid small talk with the other guests.

Our conversation moves across the innocuous terrain of shared tastes in music, the latest movies, how beautiful Bologna is, the gay and lesbian center at Cassero, the porticoes, until, in an unpredictable shift to a more personal topic, he confides: "Two years ago my best friend committed suicide. He was like a brother to me. I've been pretty depressed ever since."

I can hardly believe my ears.

This is the first time I've met anyone who's had an experience like mine and spoken openly about it.

"My ex hanged himself a few months ago," I say.

We are two survivors who have just met on this desert island of people who are drinking, laughing, and dancing.

Now we can see each other.

Now we really see each other.

We recognize each other.

"Then you know what I'm going through."

"Perfectly."

We spend the rest of the evening immersed in conversation. We tell each other everything about our personal tragedies, even the details that we usually hide from others out of either discretion or shame. Any reticence between us would be pointless.

Talking with him is better than talking to a therapist or psychic.

Finally, someone who understands me without my having to explain everything.

His name is Alberto.

He's in Milan for the weekend, the guest of the friend who introduced us. He's going back tomorrow afternoon.

When the time comes to say goodbye, he says, "We haven't even exchanged numbers."

And we don't, since we both know how to get them anyway.

On Monday night he calls.

"I want to see you again," he says.

I answer, naturally, "Me, too."

I join him in Bologna the following Saturday. We pick up our conversation where we left off.

"It's like a neon light that stays on all the time. Other people can turn it off, not you. It will stay on forever and little by little the light will fade, or you'll simply get used to it, which may as well be the same thing. And what seemed to be monstrous and intolerable at first will instead become part of your everyday reality and you will gradually learn to accept it."

A neon light that is always on: No one had ever given me such an accurate picture of what I was feeling.

Alberto does not offer me consolation. He offers me believable scenarios. He shows me the footsteps of someone who has already traveled this path.

Alberto is three years older than me. Short hair, a beard. A massive body. Now he's in sales, but for many years he worked at an important local radio station, as the director and a DJ. I can tell he has the perfect voice for the job. Maybe his conversation resonates deep inside of me because of the tone, so calm and steady, with which he tells me things.

He tells me that a girl once fell head over heels for him just by listening to him on the radio. That she started to wait for him outside the station, bringing him gifts. How embarrassing it was to have to reject that gentle and determined courtship.

I understand the girl. The appeal of his calm, deep voice. It's soothing just to listen to him.

When he drives me back to the station, we kiss as we say goodbye.

The next night he calls me.

"You don't have to say anything, but I want you to know that I am falling in love with you."

I don't have to say anything, but I do: "Thank you."

How can someone fall in love with me in the state that I'm in? But it's as if he sees through and beyond me.

He books a hotel room the following weekend.

Spending the night with him means making love to another person again.

I wonder if I'm capable.

I find out that I am. In one way or another.

I also discover that he is patient. That in the back of his mind he knew he had to be.

And so we begin to see each other.

I join him in Bologna on weekends. He shows me around the city and introduces me to his friends. We go on walks under the porticoes and spend long afternoons in record shops, one of the passions that we have in common.

The more I get to know Alberto, the more I like him. I'm aware of this, but my head is somewhere else half the time, while my heart is a dark, shrunken, inviolable organ.

These weekends are like a spin of the roulette wheel. Sometimes I manage a semblance of serenity, but other times it's a disaster, with me forcing him to stay in the car with me for half an hour at a time while I cry and cry, unprovoked.

Even in our intimacy I'm moody, swinging between moments when I can let myself go and others when I don't want to be touched.

Despite this emotional schizophrenia, we continue on, I don't know how.

Sometimes it's Alberto who comes to Milan to stay with me.

Which means staying with me in that apartment.

How many guys would have had the courage?

But it doesn't scare him. He's not afraid of the dark because he's been close to it himself. He lets me face my fears in the place where I've chosen to face them.

He can't imagine how much I appreciate him for that.

The first time we go to the movies, we choose neutral territory (science fiction). No love stories, no dramas, nothing too romantic, nothing too realistic.

Space, aliens, mysteries, adventure: On paper it looks like a safe choice.

And instead (destiny can be so perfidious), about halfway through the film, one of the crew members has a crisis, is distraught, feels sick. The others notice he is missing and find him in his little cabin. On the screen all we see are his feet dangling from above.

I can feel Alberto paralyzed by my side.

"Let's get out of here," he says.

I'm motionless, my hands are gripping the armrests as if at any moment my seat could be shot into space.

The scene carries a shock that is powerful and vacuous at the same time.

He insists, "Let's leave."

"No, it's over now," I say. And it's true, the film has already moved on (alien battles, emergencies amid the stars).

"Are you sure?"

I am. All that scene did was remind me of what I'm always thinking. Nothing to be upset about.

Alberto is more shaken than I am. Poor guy. He had hoped to take my mind off of things, to take me to another dimension for a couple of hours.

"It's not a problem, really," I reassure him.

Not even outer space gives me enough distance. My personal tragedy is echoed even light-years away.

The screen seems to be asking me: Where did you think you were running away to, you idiot?

London is always pleasant. Every time I go, I find something new and interesting to do. I also have a few friends who live there. Not to mention the theaters, markets, record shops, and bookstores. A week in London is a perfect vacation. When Alberto suggested it, I was happy to accept.

I thought that when I got there, I would find the energy I needed, that the vibrant atmosphere of the city would rub off on me. Not to mention that I was going with Alberto, for our first vacation together.

I was fooling myself. I wanted to fool myself.

Being a tourist requires energy and interest. The moment we landed on British soil, I realized I had neither.

What I was able to do was acquiesce to whatever Alberto wanted. If he proposed a trip to Camden, I'd go along, following him like a shadow among the booths. Want a hamburger at a diner in Soho? Sure, I'd accept, and then eat only a third of my burger and pick at a couple of french fries. He would talk, comment on things, go into shops, walk through a park. I was by his side, silent and miserable.

His efforts to cheer me up were all in vain. In compensation for my apathy, he was trying to be enthusiastic for both of us.

I felt like I was dragging a dead weight behind me. Steeped in darkness, even my clothes weighed me down. Every step required a monumental effort.

To think that I was ready for a trip like this, a vacation for two, was an epic fail.

The rain, the sunshine. The little restaurants. Navigating between one line of the Tube and the other. Lying on the grass on Primrose Hill while children frolicked and shrieked around us.

Exhausting, the whole business was exhausting. The sheer effort of watching the sunset.

One afternoon, in an extreme attempt to get me excited, he told me to follow him, without revealing where he wanted to take me. He was taking me to a tattoo parlor that we had walked past a couple of days earlier. In the window there were prints with elaborate designs, silver skulls and studded straps, framed photos of tattooed thighs and forearms, scrolls with Japanese ideograms, metal jewelry, and two unfolded angel wings: the whole spectacle set on a red velvet cloth. Half of the shopwindow was covered with 1930s-style adhesive letters spelling out "Tattoo Studio." Alberto had stopped to gawk at the array, but I thought he was just being curious. Now instead he revealed his intentions: "I want to get a piercing through my right nipple."

I looked at him in amazement. "You're crazy."

"I'm not, I've been wanting to do this for a long time. I can do it here, as a souvenir of our trip."

In all its violence, it was a romantic gesture.

I let him go in alone. I didn't feel like accompanying him inside and witnessing.

Not even that small favor did I grant him.

Grief can make you selfish. Stupid. As if my heartbreak and I were the only things on earth. Don't ask us for anything.

That same night, in our hotel room, Alberto announced that he'd had enough.

"I can't take this anymore. I thought a vacation would be good for you. But it's not, you're too distant. You're lost, your mind is always somewhere else. It makes no difference to you if I'm by your side. On the street you don't even look around, you just move along with your head down as if you were on your way to work. You barely open your mouth."

He was right. He was right about everything.

"I know it's not your fault, but I'm tapped out. It makes no sense to continue on like this: Let's break up."

The first thing I felt, when he proposed breaking up, was relief. I would no longer have to put on a fake smile, walk around the city sightseeing, performing the obligatory role of a tourist on a pleasure trip. I could return freely to my torments.

Yes, thank you, yes.

I told him he was right, that it made no sense to go on like this.

We didn't need to argue. Not that there was much to say.

Then something happened.
Alberto fell asleep, exhausted.
I couldn't sleep a wink.

Sitting in the dark, in bed, the light from streetlamps peeking through the blinds, our clothes draped over the chairs, the noise of traffic on the street at night. And me, thinking and understanding.

I realized with absolute clarity that I had reached a crossroads: On the one hand, to surrender to grief again, wrap myself in the now familiar blanket of malaise, that obfuscating layer that for months had separated me from the world, putting me in a place where nothing and no one could reach me; and on the other hand, Alberto, life. The future.

I asked myself what I wanted.
I asked myself: Do I want to go on living?

I could feel the tentacles of despair brushing against me, enticing me with their black slime, wrapping around me with warmth and reassurance: It's us, your companions from the last few months, can you hear us? Do you recognize us? We're your everyday life, your baseline.
We are your reality.

I asked myself, again: Do I want to go on living?
And I forced myself to answer.

The next morning, when Alberto woke up, I had this absurd thing to ask. "Can you wait one more day before you leave me?"
"What's changed?"
"I've changed."
It sounded like an empty promise (who changes overnight?), a last-minute deception. But we were in a foreign city and still had a bit of vacation left, so why not enjoy our remaining time together.
He agreed, unconvinced.

But it was true. I had changed.
I had told myself: Snap out of it.

The one more day that Alberto granted has lasted for twenty-two years. And it continues today.

In the very moment I was not looking, at my lowest point, I found the love of my life.

I often think back on how much pain I unloaded on Alberto in those early months, he having just come out of his own grief and then having to shoulder mine.

Our story was born from bereavement, his own slowly dissipating and starting to overlap mine, and mine, which was still growing.

He chose to stand by me, by my sobbing, by the ghost of a man who was constantly evoked in a personal mythology forged out of guilt and remorse.

I wonder how he was able to stand it.

Our story was more like a film negative: Rather than the excitement and joy of falling in love, there were tears and crises. More like a lead weight than the exhilaration of first kisses, first dates, and first nights together.

There were good times, of course, but they required a tremendous effort on both our parts. Wobbly tightrope artists, each with his own personal burden of suffering.

We did have a prospect of happiness. One day it might happen.

And one day it did.

You never heal.
    You never stop suffering.
    You never forgive.
    You are never saved.

You choose.

Is it really possible to say no more suffering, no more, now I'm going to start living again?

I did. It was like hitting a switch. On/Off. I hit On and the light returned.

On that sleepless night, I knew I had reached a limit.

For months I had been pining over S. and his pain, the pain that had led him to the point of no return. Because of my inability to save him. I went to psychics begging for an answer, I wanted to hear that his torment was finally over, and over forever.

I raged about his right to happiness, forgetting that I, too, might be entitled to some.

Maybe we all have a limit. I had reached mine. Beyond was only the abyss. The renunciation of life.

The man who was sleeping by my side now was an amazing person, so amazing that he'd stood by me in my darkest hour, fallen in love with me when I was incapable of any form of romance. Loved me at my worst.

That, too, I had been unable to recognize.

The moment had arrived. Now or never.
The moment to save myself.

"This happens to me as it happens to everyone. You are not you for months at a time. When you can become you again, you can actually greet yourself. You can welcome yourself back."
—HEIDI JULAVITS, *THE FOLDED CLOCK*

A DIFFERENT DIMENSION

Francesca Jaks Gaffuri radiates something. I sensed it the first time I saw her in an online video, and now she is confirming it through the bright and luminous gaze that she is training on me.

If it is indeed possible to find a positive way to cope with a family tragedy, then she is living proof.

On October 5, 2011, Peter Jaks, a former champion of the Swiss national hockey team, comitted suicide by throwing himself on the train tracks near the Santo Spirito train station in Bari. He had left his home in Bellinzona three days earlier, announcing that he was going to visit his mother in the Czech Republic. Instead he headed to Italy, where he wandered aimlessly until the moment that he took his life in Puglia.

Francesca was his ex-wife. Together they had three daughters.

Ten years later, she told the story in public in an interview she gave during a live broadcast on Swiss radio. After hearing it, I decided to contact her. She immediately agreed to see me.

We meet for lunch at a restaurant in Lugano, on a pleasant, mild day. On the phone she had already said that I could ask her whatever I wanted, without qualms: In person her smile granted me the freedom.

I begin by asking her how well-known Peter was. I learned that he was quite famous in Switzerland as a great athlete and a great hockey player, a very popular sport in this country. He was celebrated and admired, by his fans, young and old.

"I have to admit that sometimes it was also unbearable for me that we were recognized everywhere, on the street, at a restaurant when we were having dinner with the family," says Francesca. "Fans were constantly erupting into our private life, there was no avoiding it."

When he stopped playing, he became the sports director of a team but lost that job. Although he was very intelligent and spoke six languages, he seemed unable to find a new position in the sports world, which sent him into a deep depression. He started gambling.

Although they had been divorced for three years, Francesca could see how unwell he was and realized that he needed help. She gave him the contact information of a psychotherapist and a toll-free number in Ticino for a group that helps gambling addicts. He promised her that he would go to the therapist.

"Sometime later he texted, 'I have an appointment on October 12.' But on October 5 he was in Puglia and..."

She doesn't finish her sentence, there's no need. Instead she tells me about the complex bond between them: "When you separate, it's because the feeling that binds a couple is gone, but that doesn't diminish the strong affection I continued to feel for him, if only for the wonderful times we spent together. We loved each other for many years."

I ask her how she felt when he died by suicide.

"I went back and forth between feeling abandoned, betrayed, and sad. My heart ached at the thought that I was so alone that I couldn't accept anyone's help. But I was also angry, because I was paying the price, basically, for a choice that somebody else had made. I think that when two people share children, they have a thread that binds them forever. Well, I felt like he had severed the thread without asking my permission."

The image of one person unilaterally severing a thread is illuminating. I can only imagine how the presence of children makes everything you have to deal with even more layered and complex.

Francesca could tell that her girls were suffering even more than she was. First because they were so young (the oldest was twenty-one, the youngest fifteen) and then because they were obviously shocked by the violence of this deed. So she set herself a goal: They would go back to living a normal life and this painful experience, rather than crush them, would become part of their existential baggage.

A titanic undertaking, in my eyes.

But she says that taking responsibility for their happiness had helped her because it gave her the strength to react and nurture them. "And three kids are a handful," she admits.

"At first the girls were angry and upset, feeling abandoned, as if they were worth nothing to their father. Getting them to understand that this wasn't true was a challenge. I'm convinced that he did it to protect us, because he was gambling, drinking, and his situation would only deteriorate. I think he wanted to spare his daughters."

Francesca seems very lucid to me, like a person who has analyzed every aspect of the situation, and for many years. Maybe this is one reason why I feel so comfortable with her, a stranger whom I feel I have known all my life.

Waiters interrupt our conversation by setting our next course on the table, but it's as if they were holograms in our perimeter. Even the food is a mere detail. We barely notice that we're eating. Sitting here at this table, forks in hand, we're in another dimension.

What makes her situation unique, however, is her husband's fame. I ask her what it meant to experience such a deeply personal grief in public.

Francesca sighs. I've hit a nerve.

"Hearing the judgments of others at a time when you are already vulnerable is very, very painful. My daughters would hear negative comments and slanderous stories about their father on TV, and they had to deal with that, too. I would always tell them, 'We have nothing to be ashamed of, it's nobody's fault, so you have to learn to accept grief, which is a part of life, and realize that our family may have a different dimension now, but we are still a family. We will always be five.'"

This woman continues to amaze me. After a separation and a suicide, I don't know how many people would say, "Our family may have a different dimension now." There is an extraordinary maturity in her point of view. For Francesca, this must be the true meaning of love.

Our meeting was made possible because we had both chosen to speak about our situation publicly. I realize that it takes time before you can reach a decision like that. Two decades in my case, one decade in hers. Yet I find it almost paradoxical that she kept silent back when the media was making insinuations and publishing falsehoods about her ex-husband, and now, so many years later, when the story might have been forgotten, she has chosen to speak about it.

"Today things are very different for me, emotionally. But I did it mainly because I think Peter's death could be of help to another person. That is my sole purpose.

When you find yourself in a situation like that, and you hear that someone else has experienced it in the exact same way, it can be so helpful for you that it would be a shame not to do anything."

I could not agree more, since that is what prompted me to write this book.

How do you feel toward Peter today?

"I only feel a great love for him, and I feel at peace. In total peace. I have learned so much from this experience. I know it might sound absurd, but it was also an opportunity for me to grow: I am no longer the woman I was ten years ago. I'm a much better person, and my daughters today are three amazing women, and I'm convinced that having had to face such a difficult situation will help them in the future. If life should bring them down again, they will know where to draw the strength to respond."

I wish there had been a whole audience of survivors with me to hear Francesca and draw inspiration and strength from her positive spirit.

In the meantime our lunch has come to an end. We ate on a patio overlooking Lake Lugano, but we've almost ignored the panorama until now. As we drink our coffee and allow ourselves to enjoy the view, Francesca indicates a spot on the coast to give me a sense of where she lives.

Then she accompanies me back to the station.

I came to Switzerland to spend not even two hours with her, and I am so glad I did.

My express train to Milan is already waiting by the platform. I am still thinking about her last answer. About the idea, which some might find inconceivable, that a tragic event like suicide can also be an opportunity for growth and improvement.

Before boarding the train, I ask her one last question: "If you were to speak with someone who has recently survived the suicide of the person they love, who is experiencing the pain of loss at this very moment, what would you say to them?"

"To deal with things one at a time. And to go easy on yourself: If you don't get something done today, it doesn't matter. You can do it tomorrow.

"I would tell them not to be ashamed, because it's absurd to feel ashamed of something like that.

"I would also tell them to seek help, not to be afraid of experiencing grief.

"And finally I would tell them to have faith, that the light will return and you will be able to enjoy life again, and in fact, something good might even come out of it.

"There is still a big taboo around suicide. But we need to talk about it. We owe it to the victims, not only to those who took their lives but also to those who are left behind. Because no one chose this, and no one lends them a hand. People like you and me need to use our story and share it with the people who need it.

"If we could help even one person, wouldn't that be fantastic?"

At this point we give each other a hug.

I started to write this book in my head more than twenty years ago. In the months following the death of S., I looked for words that I hoped would lend order to the chaos that had descended on me, give it a form, a structure. An act of mourning in the form of a novel.

In my mind I thought of the book as a way to explain what it is like to go through an experience like this. An explanation that was not for everybody. Not for general readers or members of the public. Not for people who would never have this experience. No, what I had in mind were the family members of the suicide victims, their children, fathers, mothers, husbands, and wives.

To those left behind.

To the other me's.

During that long-ago phone call I was asked a very sensible question: Are you taking notes?

Yes, I was. Even before I realized I was.

I have the stupid habit of not taking notes, which is a mistake for a writer. I am a writer without a notebook. I prefer to let my ideas percolate in my head until I feel the need to write them down. If I forget them, so be it. They obviously weren't that important.

I never stopped thinking about this book, although I kept putting it off. Every now and then I would go back to it, worried, to make sure it was still there.

It always was.

Its pages were waiting for me to start typing. Sooner or later I'll find the strength, I would tell myself.

In the meantime, decades went by.

As I'm writing these pages, now and then I come up with clichés, by automatic reflex, about how heartbreaking it all is, how wounded I felt, hurting so bad it was like tearing my skin off.

I have to go back and delete them. They're not authentic. They're commonplaces, the kind of words you might expect from someone who has experienced moments like this.

The truth is different.

Writing this book, I realize, is easy.

I sit at the keyboard and the words flow from my fingertips with absolute naturalness.

I've held these words in for far too long, imagined and shaped them, feeling them on my tongue like candy, with a hint of poison. I'm used to them. I can tolerate them.

When I was young, I used to wonder when you could consider yourself a writer, when you would allow yourself to wear that name. I thought it was connected to outside perception, to public recognition (a book with your name on the cover, landing on the bestseller list, winning an award, getting invited to literary festivals, being interviewed on TV...). I had achieved some of these goals, but I felt that there was always something more to aim for, something more important and meaningful.

With time I came to realize that you are a writer because you think like a writer. Because you stash away the things that happen to you, because you remember the names of people and places, and storylines, because you tend to recall the past in the form of stories, because you don't restrict yourself to living an experience, instead you wish to analyze it in the hope of finding a beginning, a middle, and an end, because it is through writing that you are able to make sense of things.

I am a writer because inside myself I had the certainty that I would write this book. It was never a question of if but when.

Even after producing pages and pages, I still could not admit that I was really doing it. These are just notes, I told myself. It's a rehearsal.

In order to acknowledge that I really was writing the book, I needed friends. A group of five writers that meet for dinner, at seasonal intervals, for the pleasure of being together and drinking, sometimes even drinking a lot. At the end of the meal, between the coffee and the digestif, when the conversational high has subsided and the atmosphere has become more pensive, the same question is always raised: "Are you guys writing?"

On my way to the restaurant I thought I might talk about something else, projects at various stages of development that I keep in a single folder on my desktop titled "Possible Novels." Every now and then I would open it, extract a file, and maybe add a chapter. I have at least five novels languishing in that limbo, and it would have been easy to pick any one of them and summarize it, but before that group, as if I were standing before a literary consciousness chapter of AA, I felt that it would be ridiculous to lie.

When my turn came, I told everyone that I was writing a book about an episode of my life that they did not know about. I told them which one. And I also admitted my uncertainties regarding its relationship to my first novel and in general to the idea of embarking on a text so deeply personal and so different from the lighthearted spirit of everything I had published until then. Doubts that only other writers could understand.

This sparked a debate over whether it is right to follow only our inspiration or whether we should instead stick to a path of artistic consistency. Tempers flared, and I watched with concealed amusement as my friends debated on my behalf. The tension subsided and we finished our dinner with hugs all around.

On the way home, the only thing on my mind was: So it's true, you will finish.

This time there was no turning back.

I'm in the newsroom of the TV station where I work nowadays and a colleague who is filling out a document asks me the date. I tell him and then I suddenly realize: It's one day after the anniversary of S.'s death.

I'm surprised because of what this means: That yesterday, I forgot.

In the early years, even the days leading up to the anniversary made me ill. An awful anniversary, the birthday of a nightmare. I could almost feel it in the air.

The impact softened as the years went by, but it was still an important and tragic date to commemorate.

But now (and while I'm writing this book!) the day has come and gone without my remembering it. Though I know this might sound contradictory, it isn't for me. It means that, like many other aspects of this story, everyday life has come to prevail over the symbolic. The thought, the memory of S., is so present and diffuse that the recurrences, the objects that belonged to him, and the earthly traces of his existence have lost their value.

Forgetting the anniversary of his death is not a failure on my part; it is an achievement.

"I remember thinking: There will come a time when I will not be thinking of this. And I was right. And I was wrong."

—AMY HEMPEL, "CLOUDLAND"

In the end, I did not reread the notebook with the letters that he left me.

I didn't have the strength.

I know that they were letters of recrimination and forgiveness, of reflection and shared memories, of regret. Streams of consciousness. A final portrait of him.

I don't know what effect it would have on me to go through it again. I fear it would be devastating.

They remain an incendiary treasure locked in a drawer to contain the flames.

I am not so naïve as to think this is a solution, a recipe. To find another person to love who loves you back.

It's pathetic to even write that.

In a situation like this, nothing is linear and clearcut, there is no formula or method. No medicine. No secret.

As in, I'll reveal the trick.

There, mystery solved.

No. That's not how it works.

Everyone has to find their own way, their own time. Their own methods. Actually, since none are available, they'll have to improvise. Deal with things as they come, and when it feels right. No matter how much affection might surround them, in the end they have to go it alone. There is no other way.

Some find solace in religion, some in therapy, some bury themselves in their work, some make their children the reason for living, some make a radical move, changing city, friends, life.

It's only right if you are doing what you feel you have to do.

Apart from the journey and the means of getting there, one thing remains essential: At some point you have to allow yourself to move on.

You have to forgive yourself.

No, we did not save him.
>We were unable to.
>We didn't understand how serious the situation was.
>We didn't catch the signs.
>We didn't believe his threats.
>We were unable to understand how deep his malaise was, and even when we did, we did not know how to address it.
>We were not always present.
>We were not omnipotent.

We might come to terms with our limitations once and for all. One way or another, we will continue to do so. But if we want to go on living, one day we will have to take pity on ourselves.

I haven't done a lot of drugs in my life. As an adult, yes, fully conscious of what I was doing, and only in social circumstances. At gigantic discotheques, usually outside of Italy, at former theaters in Amsterdam with three levels of balconies, abandoned factories in Berlin, underground clubs in Brussels, tensile structures on the outskirts of Madrid, surrounded by hundreds of half-naked men drenched in sweat who seemed to be moving in sync with me, a wet welcoming mass of humanity as far as the eye can see, moving to the rhythm of the thundering bass emanating from the speakers, as if we were inside a giant beating heart.

Moments of chemical and cosmic bliss, vibing with the world, with life, with my species. And every time, every single time, in those moments when the spirits and the flesh are exalted, I have a thought for S. I send him a prayer, as pure as can be, secular and stoned.

May you be happy, S., I hope you really have found peace, I know that I have with Alberto, all of this must mean something, I hope it does, and one day I might understand, I will never stop hating you but above all I will never stop loving you, may you be happy, S., wherever you may be.

ACKNOWLEDGMENTS

There are many people whom I feel I should thank for this book.

To the friends who read it and offered their opinions and encouragement, even when I did not know if I would be able to complete it, especially Antonella, Giorgio, and Paolo. To Riccardo, who allowed me to use his words.

To the professionals who shared with me their experience, a small part of which has flowed into these pages: Maurizio Pompili, Denise Erbuto, and Giada Maslovaric.

To Francesca Jaks Gaffuri, for her extraordinary testimony.

To Monica, who from the beginning made me feel understood and protected.

To my parents and my sister, who stood by me in the darkest period.

To all those who, in so many different ways, offered me their support when I really needed it.

And, of course, to Alberto, who may not read this, but that's okay, too.

Epigraph Credits

Page vii: *Mr. Know-It-All: The Tarnished Wisdom of a Filth Elder* by John Waters. Copyright © 2019 by John Waters. Reprinted by permission of Farrar, Straus and Giroux. All Rights Reserved.

Page 57: *As Consciousness Is Harnessed to Flesh* by Susan Sontag, edited by David Rieff. Copyright © 2012 by David Rieff. Reprinted by permission of Farrar, Straus and Giroux. All Rights Reserved.

Page 85: *The Year of Magical Thinking* by Joan Didion, copyright © 2005 by Joan Didion. Used by permission of Alfred A. Knopf, an imprint of the Knopf Doubleday Publishing Group, a division of Penguin Random House LLC. All rights reserved.

Page 136: *On Earth We're Briefly Gorgeous: A Novel* by Ocean Vuong, copyright © 2019 by Ocean Vuong. Used by permission of Penguin Press, an imprint of Penguin Publishing Group, a division of Penguin Random House LLC. All rights reserved.

Page 155: *The Chronology of Water: A Memoir* by Lidia Yuknavitch. Copyright © 2010 Lidia Yuknavitch. Published by Hawthorne Books & Literary Arts, Portland, Oregon, 2011.

Page 209: *The Way Through the Woods: On Mushrooms and Mourning* by Litt Woon Long, translated by Barbara J. Haveland, translation copyright © 2019 by Barbara J. Haveland. Used by permission of Random House, an imprint and division of Penguin Random House LLC. All rights reserved.

Page 224: By A. M. Homes, in *Why We Write About Ourselves*, edited by Meredith Maran. Published by Plume, an imprint of Penguin Random House, 2016. Permission to use copyrighted material granted by Meredith Maran and A. M. Homes.

Page 231: From the poem "Elegy" in *Stretching the Agapé Bra* by Steve Abbott. Published by Androgyne Press, San Francisco, 1980.

Page 269: *The Folded Clock: A Diary* by Heidi Julavits. Copyright © 2015 by Heidi Julavits. Published by Anchor Books, a division of Penguin Random House LLC, New York, in 2016.

Page 285: "Cloudland" in *Sing to It: New Stories* by Amy Hempel. Copyright © 2019 by Amy Hempel. Published by Scribner, an imprint of Simon & Schuster, Inc, in 2019.

Other Credits

Song lyrics on page 94 from "No Regrets" by Robbie Williams and Guy Antony Chambers, 1998. Lyrics on page 94 from "I Will Survive," by Freddie Perren and Dino Fekaris, 1978. Lyrics on page 95 from "Believe," by Paul Barry, Matthew Gray, Brian Higgins, Stuart McLennen, Timothy Powell, and Steven Torch, 1998.

Erik Satie quote on page 156 from *A Mammal's Notebook*, translated by Antony Melville and edited by Ornella Volta. Published by Atlas Press, London, in 1996.